LEONARD

THE

LIAR

NICHOLAS GAGNIER

For my friend N.L.

Table of Contents

Foreword by Kindra M. Austin

My introduction to Nicholas Gagnier's work was piloted by his blog, Free Verse Revolution. I was immediately taken with the potency of his informal poetry, as well as his dedication to advocate for mental health awareness. Nicholas bares the uncountable truths of the human heart; be these truths dirty and cruel, or exquisite and hopeful, his words flow like lifeblood. *Swear to Me*, released in 2017, attests to the depth of his humanity and creativeness.

Leonard the Liar is an intimate glimpse of life; it is about self-reflection, and metamorphosis. You will find that Nicholas' ability to capture the human spirit through fiction equals the effectiveness of his poetry. Rich with vulnerability, spite, and love, everyone involved in this story must make a choice. Stand and fight for truth? Walk away in defeat? Remain the same? Set someone free? These are all decisions pertinent to living.

When Nicholas asked me to write the foreword for *Leonard the Liar*, I agreed without hesitation. His friendship and continual support of my work are both beautiful, and appreciated beyond words. I admire him for his kind soul, keen eyes, and ambition to write the things that truly matter. He is among my favorite collaborators—together, we make sense out of nothing. To discover a writer like Nicholas, immune to pretentiousness, is a rare gift.

I have no doubt that Nicholas poured his entire essence into this book.

Happy reading, my friends.

Kindra M. Austin

Prologue

Twenty-four years passed before my daughter broached the origins of her given name.

I was confident, as most young parents are, the question would have come up much sooner. I thought- as she passed through the annals of adolescence, trying to hide joints in her school bag and dated boys (many of whom were of questionable character)- that she would pause a moment and look across the kitchen table, hazel burning holes in my morning paper and asking the inevitable.

"Dad?" I imagined she would say, somehow able to break the lone syllable in two and suggest the second half belonged to a higher octave.

"Yes, honey?"

"Why Skylar? Was there any point to it? Did Mom, like, find it in a baby name book or something?"

But the questions never came. When I looked over my paper, she was avoiding my gaze, eyes swimming in the cereal bowl. Over the years, she seemed to eat a little faster and leave for school a little quicker. The playful conversations at dinner were replaced by deflections and defensive conversations.

By the time I could have a sincere conversation with Skye, one that didn't include some form of omission, fib or white lie to make us feel like better parents, she was well into her twenties. Hair that used to reflect every other colour of a rainbow stabilized into a dark blonde. Makeup adopted moderation, and she wasn't stapling piercings into every corner of her face. Skye dressed sharper, paid her own way through university working with my brother Luke on weekends, and fell in love.

In some ways, she came to embody the woman we named her after.

Just not at sixteen.

It wasn't until after her mother's funeral, on a lukewarm November evening in 2034, that she finally asked me.

The days leading up to the ceremony are some of the murkiest, most mud-coloured of my life. I like to believe losing my partner of a quarter century was too traumatizing to remember.

I was fifty-five when she passed. The crinkle-free surface of my skin had stepped aside for the creases of seniority. Gray streaks were rampant. She had been sick a long time, and I was happy just to have my hair. At my age, not every gentleman could make that claim.

Looking around the church, as I presided over Claire's casket for the hundred sets of staring eyes, standing beneath flowers that tried to take our loss and cover it in something beautiful, I tried to count how many I actually knew.

I tried to listen to their eulogies, their connections to my late wife that ranged from acquaintance to mother, co-worker to student. Several of her friends, and sister

Renee, spoke.

I could only name a handful of them.

Skylar hung her head in contemplative silence. The dress she had chosen was the same one Claire had worn to her own mother's funeral. Simple black and a flowered veil to match.

Jackie Kennedy, had she been a blonde and left the shades at home.

Skylar decided to stay in Ontario a few more days. Her fiance Eric, was able to stay for the service and then headed back out West for work.

Eric is, by far, the most agreeable man my daughter ever dated. He works long hours, but treats her right and always brings cigars home with them.

I didn't mind being left alone, even now. It would not have bothered me if my daughter was unable to stay.

But Skylar, sensing I was more upset than I let on, was having none of that. We sat by two burning logs in the room we used to dwell as three, drinking French merlot; waiting in the dark to hear Claire's footsteps, the hoarse voice she developed in her later years from smoking, or the furious movements of her pen as she graded quizzes for her tenth grade class.

"It's so quiet," Skylar said.

"I think the quiet's here to stay."

"So weird, isn't it?"

"Pointing out how weird it is doesn't make it any less weird."

"Someone had to say it."

"You know," I said, "I remember we brought you home for the first time. Your Mom used to sit in that same armchair, and sing you to sleep. And what would she sing? Oh, everything. Knew the words to every song. I was lucky if I remembered two words of a line. But you name it, she knew it."

"Mom had a good voice."

"Yes, but she never sang for me. Only for you."

"Really?"

"I tried to get her to sing for me on our second date. Took her out for karaoke. She refused to get up on stage. At first I thought, maybe this girl can't sing. Maybe she's embarrassed. Whatever. It didn't matter.

"It was only a year or two later, on your Aunt Renee's birthday, that I went out with her a second time to karaoke. Your Mom said she wouldn't sing, but Renee got her to. They got up on stage, picked out some random song. Suddenly, it was like an angel was singing in front of me."

"How do you know it wasn't Aunt Renee?" Skylar asked.

"Because I know for a fact that she couldn't hit a key to save her life. Still can't. As for your Mom, I never figured out why she refused to honour my song requests. All I know is that once you were here, she had no problem at all."

"I always noticed some animosity between you and Aunt Renee. Is there a story to that?"

"My girl," I grinned, "there's a story for

everything."

"Everything?"

"Everything."

"So, the creepy bird above our mailbox?"

"Your mother found it at a flea market in Florida.
I tried to talk her out of it. What else you got?"

"The swords in the basement."

"Uncle Luke won them at a stag and doe when
he was twenty and managed to stab himself in the foot
with one at the same party. I confiscated them and have
had them ever since."

"The picture of you and the blonde girl in that
chest kicking around the attic. There's gotta be
something there."

"What picture?"

"You know; the one with the black frame that
looks like you bought it from Dollarama?"

"What's wrong with Dollarama frames?"

Skye shook her head and giggled, reminiscent of
when she was a little girl.

"You're such a guy, Dad. But, um, seriously.
Who is she?"

Did you look it up in a baby book or something?

It wasn't the exact phrasing I had in mind for my
rehearsed answer, but it was the closest my daughter
ever came.

"She's the woman you're named after."

"Skylar?"

"That's right. Mind you, the picture itself is from
college. But not a year before your mom got pregnant

with you, I ran into her again." I tried to recall what photograph she had found, and the face beside my own; shoulder-length blonde hair, eyes like an ocean just before the storm.

"'Ran' into her? You make it sound like you two hooked up in some seedy bar."

I lit a cigarette. The heat instantly soured my palate and spoiled my breath. In the fifty-odd years I had been on this planet, society had progressed from alleviating the common cold to negotiating the end of cancer but half a million people could still die of smoking-related disease every year.

"Believe it or not," I replied, "we did."

"You cheated on Mom?" The question could have easily been asked by her expression alone. Mouth agape, wide-eyed. *Kids still say the darndest things.*

"God no, child. Keep your voice down."

"Dad, that's what *hook up* means. You know? *To hook up.*"

"You'll have to forgive me. I'm out of touch with lingo the current slate of youth has taken."

"What did she want? This woman. Skylar."

I mulled on her inquiry a moment, absently pulling more smoke into my lungs but forgetting to exhale. A maelstrom of chemical bliss flooded my brain before settling to the bottom of my lungs, leaving the same dull ache I experienced almost on a daily basis. I was beginning to feel the same way about smoking I learned from hangovers after the age of thirty; that consequences suck.

"Dad?"

"Hmmm?"

"What did Skylar want?"

I paused again, lost in a different place than my child.

"She wanted to-she wanted to tell me she was dying."

"And did she?" Skylar asked. "Die?"

(*Beth will never be able to end my life.*)

"Yes."

"Oh," she said, "I'm sorry."

I shrugged.

"It's okay. Been a long time. Funny side of it is, had that sort of thing happened now, it would be nothing. She would probably still be alive."

(*You're the guy who does the right thing.*)

"So what happened, exactly?"

"Come again?" I asked, after another prolonged pause.

"What happened with all that?"

(*The right thing.*)

"That's a long story, kid, and it's late."

"I got time," Skylar replied, holding up the bottle of wine. A yellow banner stretched around its equator, stamped with a black bird against the tinted glass. The booze inside could be heard sloshing against the sides, impressively camouflaged in bottled-necked darkness. "And alcohol."

I lit another cigarette between my lips.

"It's your funeral, kid."

LEONARD

THE

LIAR

Destiny is a funny thing.

I used to scoff at the idea.

Then I met an old flame — twenty-seven days before I was supposed to marry the love of my life.

It started in a bar, of all places.

Dark and faintly scented of piss, beer and the serving wench's disposition to perfume, I often come here alone, order a Coke, and enjoy the show.

Boozers past their prime are kicking in spirit. Unhappily married men watch sports games to a backdrop of Bruce Springsteen and Janis Joplin. The singles scene consists of a few guys dropping in and out to hit up the twenty-something bartender, showing off their abs and starting fist fights.

More often than not, it ends with broken beer bottles.

Eight years of sobriety do a ton for the atmosphere, both in my head and this establishment. Other people get to drink on their problems.

I'm allowed to dwell.

"Leonard?"

At first I think it's God, come to collect on years of ignorance. I didn't think the voice would be female.

"Oh my God," it says.

Would the creature take its own name in vain?

"What has it been? Ten years?"

The stranger talking to me comes into focus. White blouse and matching jacket. Her blonde hair is longer than I remember. Fingers mourn the lack any nail extensions or polish. My eyes start at her feet. Tennis shoes.

The legs are bare, up to the shin where the skirt begins. I climb her stomach and chest, up a neckline free of jewelry. Finally, the face. It's one I recognize. Thin lips, a tight jaw and sordid gray eyes. The expression spread across this face is nothing like the last one I saw it adorn.

She's thinner; those gray eyes a little deeper in their sockets.

New Year's Eve, 2008. I was tripping balls, inhaling things I couldn't differentiate and fucking everything in sight. Funny she was the one to drop the bomb first.

"Well, holy shit," I say, "It's Skylar fucking Bates."

"You don't drink anymore?" Skylar asks, gesturing to the soda in front of me. "You know, considering we're in a bar and all."

She joins me in the booth. No invitation is needed or offered.

I clear my throat.

"Eight years sober last month."

"Wow. I mean, congratulations. Kinda figured you might have drank yourself into early grave by now."

"I'm getting married, actually."

"Bullshit."

"June sixteenth."

20

"This from the man who epitomizes bachelorhood. You're serious?"

I chuckle.

"What can I say to convince you?"

"Nothing! I don't mean... I'm so happy for you!" Fumbling words. "You always needed someone to bring order to your life, Len. This is totally great. Your problem was always keeping enough blood in your head long enough to acknowledge it."

"I take it you're congratulating me in your own, weird way,"

"Definitely. This is a good thing."

"Thanks," I reply.

"How's your brother?"

"Luke's good. Deciding whether getting married was worth it, years after the fact."

"Is he still over-the-top?"

"Of course, Have to say, though, if you thought Luke was over-the-top, you should meet his wife."

"Why?" Skylar asks. "Is she mean?"

"Mean doesn't even begin to describe Monica. She jabs needles of ink into people for a living. Looks the part, too. The other day, I told her she couldn't have been endowed with a more suitable profession. To which she replied I should soak my head in a pot of boiling water."

"How do you put up with someone like that?"

"It's simple," I reply, "They love each other. There's got to be something there; it's gone on this long. So we...tolerate her."

"You still let shit roll off you, don't you?" she says, "Never getting confrontational? Out the door the first chance you get. I'm just like you, Leonard. We made the most dysfunctional pairing, but of all the men in my life, you made the most sense."

"You're not about to propose an ultimatum, are you? That might be a little weird for me."

"Don't flatter yourself, sir."

"What about you?" I ask. "Surely you must be up to no good these days."

She hesitates. A breath held too long escapes her. It's funny, to see an ex-flame's quirks ten years in, just the way you left them. Restless hands. Holding breath. Just the way they were.

"Well, it's been a tough couple years. I don't see people anymore. Everybody grew up and got on. I'm living with my sister, but with Mom gone and my Dad in dementia, even she and I are pretty disconnected."

"What about your brother? Is he still around?"

"Todd lives in California with his girlfriend. He doesn't want to be disturbed by the thought of what's going on back home. I don't know, Len. I'm twenty-seven years old, I have no friends except my sister. The family's either dying off or writing us off. I just started thinking about what matters before it's all gone, you know?"

"What about work? That usually keeps people pretty grounded, doesn't it?"

Skylar shrugs.

"I don't have a job. Anymore. I spend some time wandering downtown, just taking in the sights. Television lost its allure months ago. Night in with a movie is not enough these days. Mostly I just...hope to find people I used to know. Re-connect with something. Whatever. I'm beyond the point now."

"What are you talking about?"

She fidgets in her seat.

"Leonard, do you ever think about fate?"

I shake my head.

"Claire brings it up from time to time but I'm not big on the soul-searching. Why?"

"The truth is, I've been trying to find you for a while. It's no coincidence we ran into each other tonight."

I struggle to understand her words, as delicate as they are. I try and rationalize them but can't.

My brain makes a connection it's been searching for.

"Be honest with me about something, okay?" I ask.

She bites her lip.

"Have you been following me lately? Calling me?"

For the past two weeks, someone has been phoning the house at different times of day. Middle of the day, middle of the night. During Sunday dinner with my brother and Monica. At first I thought nothing of it. More recently, a black car started parking across from our building. Claire was hysterical for three days. Then it stopped,

She still spent Friday night periodically peering out the window.

Eyes look down and to the left.

I lean forward in my seat, almost spitting the words.

"Are you crazy? My fiancee thought you were a stalker, Skylar!"

"Leonard," she says, "I'm sorry. I was just waiting for the right time. I wouldn't have done it if I'd known it was going to freak you out like this!"

"What the hell did you expect?"

"I don't know, Len! I really needed to talk to you, okay?"

I fall back in the booth.

"I have to go."

"Leonard, *please.*"

"I just want to walk away."

"I need your help," she pleads. "I'll do anything.

Just hear me out."

Anger takes hold, zero to ten inside a second. With shaking hands, I grab my vacated chair by its backrest, slamming it into the floor beneath. Cheap wood shudders at the impact.

"You listen to me. In less than a month I'm getting married. Whatever happened between you and I is *over*. No more phone calls. Don't come to my house. Stay away from Claire. Stay away from me. Understand?"

"Leonard, please. It's not like -"

This is not your problem. This is not your problem. This is not your problem...

"No more, Skye. If I see you again, I'm calling the police."

I release my grip on the chair. Without giving her a chance to explain- what could she possibly have to say?- I make for the door by the bar.

The world is a blur in all my unchecked rage.

The cursor keeps blinking.

Under a dim glow, the room feels colder than it should. Bumps in the night are amplified. Little snaps and crunches of the keyboard are louder. Intimately rehearsed conversations project themselves on the page; a killing spree of white space.

Times like this, I think of my parents.

Luke and I were home when we got a call from the Toronto General. I caught the news segment in the OR waiting room. A middle-aged woman, living illegally in the country as a housekeeper at the time, was collecting her employer's twins from Girl Scouts. My parents had gone to a doctor party- Dad was a neurosurgeon- and gotten trashed. Nobody thought to take my father's keys away from him.

Mom and the housekeeper were pronounced dead on arrival. The police told me my mother failed to do up her seat belt and was subsequently crushed under the car. A closed casket was recommended to us. We cremated both of them. Dad clung to life almost a week, unable to speak, unable to communicate in his agony. Doctors scrambled to find the bleeding source, performing every emergency surgery they could muster.

It wasn't enough.

"Leonard?"

There's a knock on my office door.

"Hey you," I say, "Come in."

Claire enters, a pink house robe loosely tied around her waist and matching slippers. Fingers brush strands of shoulder length blonde to the back of her ear. Blue eyes stare back at me. She walks up behind my chair, wrapping arms around me in a tight embrace. Her head rests on my shoulder, leaving a kiss down my neck.

"Everything OK?"

"Sure," I reply, "Why?"

"You've been in here a while."

I lift my arm, using my palm to smooth creases out of my forehead. My corneas are fixated on one sentence riding on the waves of white pixels. There's space for so much more. There's room for my wedding vows, which I've struggled for months to write, a Leviathan of sentiment in itself. There's real estate to cover how I feel about my encounter with Skylar Bates days earlier, but I don't dare leave a paper trail.

"Just trying to find an an entry point back into my head."

"How long have you been at it?"

"About four hours now."

"Well," she says, taking a seat in my lap, "I can think of about four things which sound more appealing, and we have to be naked for about three and a half of them."

Blue eyes, staring back at me like a starving

mountain lion.

She's on the prowl.

"Mind telling me for which half I get to keep my clothes on?"

Claire grins.

"Why don't you come to the living room so we can decide if you get to keep anything?"

Taking my hand, she leads me to the hall and past the bedroom, our queen bed of a hundred throw pillows never considered. Blue walls of our hallway, adorned with picture frames, pass by like a beautiful day.

I drive her toward the couch but she wants the floor.

"Still want to know what I get to keep," I say with a grin.

"Shut up and take your pants off."

We're kissing, touching; exploring familiar territory that feels new every time. Nails break skin on my back, and her robe falls away. She tears at my clothes, between our flesh, hunger overtakes higher function.

Her hips sway as the rest of her body rises and falls with each sensation. Tips of my fingers run from her navel to her nipples. All throughout, ice-blue eyes stare up at me between the intervals she can't keep them open. I reciprocate with my hips pushing against Claire's legs, our bodies pressing against one another, minds and bodies in sync for almost an hour.

"That was amazing," Claire says, falling flat on

her back with me, staring up at a constellation of ceiling mould.

"God, I was so worried you were going to complain."

Claire turns her head to look into my eyes.

"In a month we'll be married, Len."

"I know," I say, "Excited?"

She turns her body inward, burrowing her head into my arms; my fingernails run up and down her back. Warm breath spills into my skin, her naked frame pressed against my taller one, legs brushing against mine.

"Are you?"

"Not fair. I asked you first."

"I stopped playing that game in third grade, you loser."

"Oh, hurtful!"

Claire's grin stretches to both ears.

"You can take it," she says. "Or maybe you can't?"

"You are right. I'm completely offended."

A pause lingers before a change in subject.

"How was work today?" I ask.

"Oh, you know. Kids excited to be getting out for summer. Driving me up the wall."

"I don't know how you do it, sweetheart."

She smiles.

"I told them we were getting married, and a fight broke out," she replies, "Seven year old boys fighting over their teacher. Imagine."

"If you were my teacher, I'd want to do you."

"It's different, Len. You're my boyfriend. An adult, or so I like to think."

"Every second-grade boy has a crush on their teacher. You're hot."

She rolls onto her back again, staring up at the popcorn ceiling, a million thoughts caught between her gears.

"They are just starting to learn basic multiplication tables and cursive handwriting, for God's sake. They're socialized in homes that know divorce and misery and they're coming to school. Some of them just... *unleash* this anger on other students.

"I had to break up a fight during recess this morning. This kid, Stevie Boyd from Bonnie's class down the hall? He attacked one of my guys. When they brought Stevie to Robert's office, we asked why he hit Abdullah." She cringes. "God, he had the most terrible smile on his face, Len."

I lean my weight on my elbows and look down on her.

"Well, what did the kid say?"

"Stevie told Robert he believes Abdullah is a terrorist, or he's going to grow up to become one. Said he was going to be responsible for killing everyone. Abdullah was terrified. Bloody nose, black eye. Lots of crying. I had Bonnie take both classes to the library so I could sit with him in the nurse's office."

"What's gonna happen to Stevie?"

She shakes her head.

"The school board is still deciding, but they sent both boys home until Monday until they can make a formal decision."

"Abdullah too? He didn't do anything wrong."

"They said it's because he was involved in a fight, but there won't be a penalty in his file."

"Just want him to recuperate, eh?"

"Exactly. I met Stevie's parents. I mean, I try not to be judgmental of the situations these kids are in, try not to take it personally, you know? But the dad was just an *asshole*. He didn't think his kid had done anything wrong. Put him in his son's place, trade the school for a bar, he might have done the same thing."

Hunching over, I kiss her forehead.

"It can't be easy, sweetheart."

I don't really have a better answer to give.

No one would notice a girl like Skylar Bates enter the Cinematica store through its stainless steel turnstile at eight-thirty on a Friday night. She's no taller or less pretty than any of the other blonde thirty-somethings who shop here, in this relic of entertainment past, on the arm of a guy roughly twice their size.

She's no less harried than the mother tapping her foot with arms crossed in the children's video section, or any more relaxed than the guy covertly browsing softcore porn in the drama section.

The staff offer her their standard, monotonous "hello". Nothing more, nothing less.

It only took a few months as the manager of this particular movie store, with its ever-flickering sign outside that sputters through each day with only half the brand illuminated, to realize its owners are not all that interested in its success or failure. Another month to account for all the holes in the ceiling, and yet another to learn that the store was bleeding money left, right and sideways.

But I slug away here every day to finance an apartment I can barely afford, and a dream to one day write something worth reading. Arriving at seven a.m daily to do the work of two people and get the store open by nine, I may well be the only member of management.

Even my assistant manager Pete, a lanky fellow with a crooked nose who always seemed to be stoned or hungover, doesn't seem to value his future in this store much.

The routine is the only thing that keeps me sane. It's a warm little fire in a cold world, one that offers heat and comfort as I have struggled to keep this little shack afloat.

From seven to eight, I get to pour over paperwork and financial logs, manipulating expenses and endlessly revising the schedule until I have to post it, only to get flack later from someone about a screwed-up availability.

From eight to nine, check in returns, dust shelves, straighten the new releases and mop the floor my wonderful employees neglected the night before. At quarter to, there's a small fist knocking on the front door. It's either Veronica, a twenty-year old girl with long black hair and more metal in her face than a desk has screws; or Mandy, a slightly taller version of Veronica, only her earlobes are the sole visible piercings she has and her every other word is not a variant of "fuck".

This morning, to my odd relief, it's Veronica knocking.

"Thanks, boss," she says, as I lock the door behind her. "Sorry I'm late. My mom was being a pain in my ass, my son is fucking constipated again, and my bus was ten goddamned minutes late."

"You're early, actually. Three minutes."

She grins, unveiling the newest addition to her repertoire of studs and rings. Under the top lip, a small circular bar hangs over the front teeth.

"New piercing?" I ask.

"Yeah. Do you like it?"

"I swear, your face is going to deflate someday. Like a balloon. Now go put your stuff away. We have a visit from Darryl and Chris today. The store has to look perfect."

I enter the narrow service counter passage- what we lowly serfs refer to as a "boat". Four computers, technological dinosaurs running on blue screens and MS-DOS in a world of smartphones and tablets, double as functional equipment. Stacks of DVD cases clutter the counter behind me.

Veronica yawns.

"Darryl and Chris? Are we still being run by those two douchebags?"

"Like their dad before them. They're our bosses and we want to impress them with all the hard work we do around here."

"You mean, you want them to be impressed with you."

"Hey," I interject, "we're a team."

"They don't care, you know? You could fucking destroy the place and they'd just piss on the debris. The only one around here who cares is you, Len."

For a girl whose height barely exceeds five-two in heels, Veronica is sharper than some knives in Claire's cutlery drawer.

"That's precisely the reason I care. If I didn't, who would?"

"I thought I already answered that question, boss," Veronica retorts.

"And I thought I told you to put your coat away.

We open in less than a minute."

"Please," she says, straightening her back and separating her arms from the blue counter. "We could be closed for a week and no one would notice."

"Chris and Darryl would care. Now go."

"Right. How else would they eat? And by the way," she says, walking away without turning her head back, "you should really spend more time with your wife, huh?"

I know better to argue with her, because she has disappeared from sight by the time I can formulate a worthy response to her challenge. Instead, I walk to the door, turn the old iron knob- the hinges squeak when the door is touched, so their angry reaction to the pressure of the lock is unsurprising- granting access to a civilization that wants nothing to do with us.

I return to my place behind the counter like a drone at heart.

This place really is going to shit.

"Okay gang," I sigh, peering out over my clipboard, "we got reamed today. Now I know Darryl can be generally unpleasant-"

"You mean a complete ass?" Veronica interrupts.

"Can I finish, Veronica?"

Veronica smacks gum between her lips, arms crossed.

"As you were, boss."

"Thank you. Pete? Look alive, would you? This is only your job we're talking about."

My assistant manager, who sits across from me, top three buttons of his blue dress shirt undone and the ends untucked, with red hair that hasn't likely met a comb it liked in months, makes a minimal effort to sit up in the grey folding chair.

The rest of my employees, mostly teens with nothing to spend their money but paying strangers outside liquor stores to supply them forty-ounce bottles of Fireball to drink in metered parking lots after closing house, look equally unimpressed.

"As I was saying, I know Darryl is not my best friend, and it's even less likely he's yours, but he's our boss and he made some very good points. The new release shelves can be dusted more, and the Coke fridge could be stocked more than once a day."

"We're the only ones who drink it, Len," Kyle says. Seventeen, with dirty blonde hair and a face only his mother and slutty kids at the mall could love.

"Let's not forget the only reason you work here," Veronica says to him, "is because Darryl is not only a jackass but your Uncle. *Which*, if my math is right, makes you a jackass. Jackass."

"Leave him alone, Veronica," Mandy spits from my right.

"Shut your whore hole, Mandy."

"Excuse me?"

"C'mon," Veronica replies, "I'm not stupid. All these guys who take you out on your lunch break. There's a new one every week. Every week!"

"*Hey*," I interrupt, "A little professionalism here, please?"

Across from me, Pete is slowly descending into a coma.

"Oh, Mandy's professional, alright. The world's oldest profession!"

"Veronica, I don't want to have to tell you again-"

Before I have formulated an assertive end to that sentence, Mandy leaps from her chair, swinging her fist into Veronica's jaw. Both girls land sideways on the floor. Kyle starts chanting *girlfight! girlfight!* Pete is briefly broken from his daze.

The other three knights of this dysfunctional round table- Kara, Nassim and Charlie- share a collective gaping jaw as Veronica prepares her counter attack. Mandy readies herself for subsequent swings.

"*Enough!*" I yell.

The room falls silent. Mandy hangs over the smaller girl, fist cocked, its delivery frozen in time. Only Kyle reacts with an ounce of fear, his eyes darting between panting co-workers and I. Not another sound or scowl is made.

I look down at the clipboard, the sole flagship of order amidst this clusterfuck of a career choice, and maybe the only sign that order survived. It only offers checklists and bullet points.

"Veronica," I say, "I'd like you to wait for me in front of the store. Outside. I will be there in ten minutes. I'd also like everyone else to leave the room except for Mandy. Kara and Kyle, go back to work. The rest of you can go home for the day."

Veronica is first out the door. One cheek might be a darker shade of red as the point of impact begins to swell, but there's equal anger in both. Kara and Kyle, dressed in their green uniform shirts and black slacks, follow her. Nassim, an olive-skinned man in his thirties, wraps his pack around one shoulder and makes a swift exit. Pete, dragging his feet, makes up the line's end.

I shut the door behind them.

"Look, Leonard, I'm sorry but she crossed a line. We both know it."

"I know," I reply, reclaiming my swivel seat in front of the dial-safe. Finally, I feel safe to let go of the clipboard, my mast in a storm. It clatters on the desk.

"I don't know how you haven't fired her yet," she says.

"Coming from the woman who just assaulted her- on company property, no less- that's slightly hypocritical, isn't it?"

There's a knock at the door, and never a moment of peace. I beckon Mandy to open it, burying my head in both hands.

"Leonard?"

"What is it, Kara?"

The large girl looms in the doorway, trying to see past Mandy's head to make eye contact with me. "There's some woman here to see you."

"Claire?"

Kara shakes her head, curled locks moving side to side. "No. Not Claire. Customer, maybe?"

"Great," I groan, "Probably the lady with the sky-high return fees. It's fine. I'll be out in a minute."

"Okay. But it's not that one, either. I know because last week, she tried to throw her sandwich over the counter at me, and I said, 'Ma'am, why did you do that?', and she said, "Because I shouldn't have pay return fees when it was returned'-"

"Thank you, Kara," I say, gesturing to Mandy to close the door. When we are alone again, I already know what Mandy is going to say.

"It's her or me, Leonard."

I groan again. "See, now I don't understand why you kids don't get along. Instead, you have to make it my fucking problem. So here's what I'm going to tell you-"

"Work together or, there's the door?"

I shrug. "Essentially. Look, I don't get paid enough to care about your drama, or her baby mama fucking attitude. I got wrecked today, Mandy. For people who have no interest in this Dumpster fire of a business, I'm tired of getting the shit end of the stick here."

"Oh come on," Mandy replies. "You do it for the customers, Leonard."

"Fuck customers. Each one is more stupid than the last. You can get Netflix at home for twelve bucks a month, and you still come here?"

"Must be the personal touch you offer."

I chuckle, having evaded her longing stare so far, a mistake I'm determined not to repeat. A mistake I know she wants me to make.

"We can't keep doing this, Mandy."

Her turn to groan, pacing back and forth- a process which, in the context of this office, is two or three steps at a time.

"Still afraid I'll tell Claire?"

"Not the point," I reply. "I just don't want to. Anymore."

"Oh," she says, in barely more than a whisper. "So you can fuck me, what? Three times?"

"We never slept together."

"Dry humped?"

"Made out. Over a year ago. Before I was engaged. Claire and I, we weren't a 'thing' yet."

"Lucky I was of age, eh?"

"You're talking about a hypothetical scenario. I stuck my dick in nothing. You shoved your tongue down my throat and were eighteen."

"Maybe I wasn't."

I don't have time for this.

"I Xeroxed your driver's license when I hired you. I can fucking say that because that, right there, next to you is a Xerox machine."

She laughs. "Everything in this dump is so old, my grandparents have lapped it. My Geemaw, she's only 51. Got herself a smartphone the other day."

"And you're two months shy of twenty," I say. "It's not happening, Mandy. I'm sorry. And I really hope we don't have to keep having this conversation." Hoping to stave off silence that only serves to thicken the hot air, I speak when she does not.

"Do you have anything else to add to this," I say, determined to escape the stuffiness of this room, "that does not consist of blackmail or guilt?"

She doesn't respond.

Following her as she grabs her purse and exits onto the ugly blue carpet that runs the length of the public area, I try to keep my eyes to the ground, ignoring the glares of my staff. Dispirited customers browse through ailes of plastic cases, oblivious to my personal Hell. I'm trying to be ready for anything else thrown at me today.

When I lift my head at the boat, close to the exit as I'll be allowed today, I realize how unprepared I am.

Skylar Bates' eyes, gray as the sidewalk outside, follow Mandy as she passes through dual metal detectors and out the chiming doors.

I would have much preferred the return fees lady.

Skylar looks back at me, seemingly older than she was days earlier.

"I know that look," she says with a wry grin.

"What did you do?"

"Skylar, what are you doing here?"

"Leonard, I really need to talk to you."

Jesus, what did I do to deserve today?

"Just five minutes."

"Look, Skye," I say, "I'm sorry about snapping on you the other night, just...well, I'm really busy today, okay? I have my own problems."

She looks around us. In the boat, Kyle is texting. Kara is, bless her heart, trying to do everything and annoyed at Kyle for slacking. There are three customers in the store and a brown mouse running between the aisles. My employees named him Popcorn and we can't get him to leave.

"Hmmm," she says, "Jam packed, it seems!"

"The sarcasm is not necessary," I reply. "What do you want?"

"Five minutes."

"Five minutes?"

"Alone."

"Fine," I say, "Come into my office. Follow me."

Between Skylar stalking me and Mandy coming onto me, I'm not sure who I'm the more furious with.

"Okay," I say, closing the door behind her, wanting to do the opposite and run for my life. I take a seat in my chair instead.

Her hands clasp together at the waist, like she were a young girl, about to receive communion, head bowed.

"What the hell is going on?"

Ten years gone. What is so important now?

Her chest rises and falls.

"I'm dying, Leonard."

"That's why-"

Her voice wavers before ironing out. Eyes traverse various shades of her gray, sadness to fury to struggle to understanding.

"That's why I've been trying to talk to you. I never knew what to say, how I would say it or what your reaction would be. I think: what would *I* say to that? I don't yet know how to explain it to myself, so don't think you're alone here.

"I'm not after you for anything. I'm not after you at all, actually. That shocked me most the other night. I was happy for... a long time after you. Went to counseling, straightened my life out, realized how I'd alienated everyone who ever loved me. I had a career once, but that's not enough for me. It's not what I want to be remembered for. There's no one-I don't know-*there* anymore. Beth is wrapped up in *her* problems and I'll probably never see Todd again." She shrugs. "Dad won't remember tomorrow I told him."

"You told him?"

"Only because he'd forget by tomorrow."

"Have you told anyone else?"

"Nobody else I can tell. Not without the world finding out."

"Is that such a bad thing?"

She drifts momentarily.

"I don't really have the heart to tell them."

"Yet, you had the heart to track me down, to call my house every day and sit outside my place all night-why?"

Wandering thoughts return to me.

"Because Len," she smiles, "You were the closest thing to love I ever knew. I don't want you to be freaked out. To be fair, it would freak me out too. You're gonna get married, have kids. You'll do great. It's not necessarily what I imagined for you, but it's everything I hope for you. I just...I wanted you to know... my life was better because of our time together. Even if I didn't show it very well."

I clear my throat.

"How long did they give you?"

"Three months. Doctors said there are blood clots lodged in my brain. Three of them. And those are the ones they can find. Said it wouldn't be long before one of them hemorrhaged, led to an aneurysm. They're inoperable. They rupture, you don't come back."

"You're remarkably calm for someone who has three months."

Skylar allows herself a smirk.

"Does it hurt?" I ask.

"Headaches, sometimes. It's funny, actually. I always imagined a terminal condition would have more flair."

"Did they give you anything for it? Medications? Aspirin, even?"

"They might have," she says, "Never asked."

She scans my face for reactions; expressions I don't know how to express in real life. Not the basic quotients of sadness, happiness, anger and confusion.

Skylar wants my extremes. Rage; whether I feel her rock bottom. Euphoria. She wants to know if I'll join with her darkness, if even briefly.

"There was a time," she says, "not long ago, all I did was lie in bed. Cried aloud. Cried to sleep. Wondered what I'd done to deserve this. I tried to converse with God. Went to church. Confessed my sins and then some. Read the Bible, but there were no revelations. No grand epiphanies. No messiahs or miracles. N*othing* coming to save me.

"Naturally, I tried one delusional coping strategy after another. Made lists of things I wanted to experience before I die. I wrote down everything I could think of; even things I don't really want to do. But it doesn't change a thing. I should have done them ten years ago."

"So what are you going to do?" I ask. "I'm sorry; I'm not really good at these types of situations. I don't know what you want to hear from me."

"Yeah. Neither am I." she replies, "But I see the world in different colors now, Len. I wish there was a way I could explain that without sounding like a whack-job."

"Proving you're sane doesn't exactly top my list."

"How can I put it?" Her face lights up a second later. "Oh! I know. Three weeks ago, Bethany took me out, right? It was a club, but there was a rock band playing. New Romantics. Have you heard of them? Anyway, they did a cover of 'Freebird', and you know how much I love that song. While they were playing, I just closed my eyes, standing at the front of the crowd. I still felt like there was nobody around me. I must have been stuffed between a hundred people, Some of them smelled pretty bad. Whatever, it's not relevant.

"Point is, I started thinking what I wanted to do with the time left. Realistically, anyway. The music spoke to me, and this....*calm* spread over me. For half the song, the part where they sing, that's what I did. Just...stood there.

"In the middle of a crowd, I stopped wanting their sympathy. Cut myself off from the rest of the world like I was flicking a switch. It was amazing. When I opened my eyes, I knew something felt different. I started dancing."

"Mm. Don't you hate dancing?"

"I know, right? But fuck if I care who's watching. Just went with it. Because for all I know, I could die tomorrow. Cherry on the cake? Everyone standing on the sidelines started dancing with me. I'd never done anything like that before. Even the band got really into it. I turned a little group of people into something."

Another pause as she hangs onto the moment.

"I thought it would be easy to confront you. Tell you what I'm not able to say to the people in my life. At least, *easier.* I hoped we would have the right amount of emotional distance between us. That words could roll off my tongue like this is nothing." She licks chapping lips. "I was wrong about that part."

Death is the ultimate break-up. It's my experience no relationship has a "good" end. Even the most mutual are momentarily uncomfortable. It's not such a stretch the end of every life operates unto the same mantra.

We stand and say goodbye, exchange numbers. There is so much I want to ask her but I don't know what the questions are. There is so much I want to say if only I knew what to talk about. Skylar leans forward and kisses my cheek before she walks away, disappearing through a spinning turnstile. I stand there for a while, as if I want her to come back and quell my uncertainty; like she holds all the answers to the world I don't have.

The bright lights emanate an obnoxious red, yellow and white glow. A visual overload is stitched into every corner of the travelling carnival. Kids infest any given intersection. Games booths are commanded by charismatic university students over loudspeakers.

Carnies are sheriffs of this lawless little land, long as they're not smoking pot or copulating with each other in alcoves underneath the roller giant coaster. Ferris Wheels and Gravitrons spin to life and slow with circadian rhythm. Shuffle people off, shuffle people on.

It's all routine.

Parents, single or otherwise, bring their offspring here in what they perceive to be a family night. It's not even close. I can hardly blame them. It's a night to set their monsters on a civilization of bells and whistles.

Teenagers travel in groups, beating the younger, less agile kids at games, contributing to anarchy any way they can. Maddening carnival music finds its way to whatever wondrous nook I find myself in, reaching peak volume somewhere along the House of Mirrors.

Skylar walks alongside me, buried in a sweater and thick glasses, having opted for sneakers over style. Her hair is tied back in a ponytail which sways from side to side. She constantly smiles at things she sees- a landed robin picking up food crumbs. A baby who lays eyes on her over a mother's shoulder.

"I'm glad you called me," she says. "I didn't expect you to, but hoped."

In return for three fucking days of torturing myself, I decided to act, dialling the digits burned into my third eye.

We arrive at the merry-go-round. Steel fences double as leaning posts for adults loitering around them, savouring a moment of peace before returning to ritualistic mollycoddling. Our fingers wrap around the horizontal bar, looking off into spinning abyss of colorful thought.

"Can I ask you a question?" Skylar asks.

"Depends on the question."

"What changed?"

"What do you mean, what changed?"

She takes a deep breath, lips pursed.

"You never struck me as the guy who'd propose."

I shrug.

"A lot changes in ten years."

"Says the man who doesn't believe in change."

"I don't know what to tell you, Skye. Somewhere along the line, it stopped being an issue. I *had* to change if I wanted to live to see thirty years old."

I hesitate.

"One night, I got hammered. *Really* hammered. I was with this girl Trisha at the time. We did a bunch of coke at her apartment and polished off a bottle of tequila. I crashed Trisha's car. Hit one vehicle, which hit another. Ended up taking out a fire hydrant. That was rock bottom. Face-deep in the airbag, a cut above my eye.

"I pushed open the door, fell to the sidewalk and puked up all over it. Passed out. Woke up in the hospital. My brother was there. My uncle was there.

Three doctors standing over me and a pair of cops.

"Crown wanted to put me away for six months but the judge didn't throw the book at me because I had a clean record. I spent two days in lockup and got sent back to rehab. When I got out, I dumped Trisha. Just stopped calling her. She came to my house once, lost it on me and walked away."

Skylar takes a moment to process. "And then you met Claire?"

I fix my gaze on the carousel with its shimmering Christmas lights in constant motion.

"I met Claire at- this is going to sound ridiculous. But, um, she mistook me for the superintendent, which was known to be a job without a person attached to it. They all kept getting fired."

Skylar says nothing.

"She had just moved in down the hall, and her pipe busted. My roommate at this time, real dick named Greg, who played guitar at three at the morning and was fucking *obsessed* with Sambuca, offered to help her on condition of a 'happy ending'."

"Oh, God," she says. "Some men."

"Anyway, there was no superintendent at the time, so I broke into the building's storage and 'borrowed' some tools. Fixed the pipe."

"You always were a rebel."

"The first time I saw Claire smile, the first time I heard her voice and it peaked in pitch as it does when she's nervous; I was at a loss. Felt like an idiot."

Skylar is silent.

"I feel like I'm talking to a wall here," I tell her.

"What do you want me to say?"

"Congratulations, Len, you're no longer the biggest fucking tool I know?"

She snickers.

"Now you're just fishing for compliments. You haven't lost that about you."

"Here I thought I was a changed man."

She bumps her shoulder to mine.

"Congrats, Len."

"Thanks. Want to start walking?"

We migrate away from the carousel, slipping back between the crowds, into anonymity. Pass the Ferris Wheel again, the game booths, the cotton candy stand housed in a commercially constructed log shack. The faint scent of popcorn filters through clear air before being pulled into the night.

Skylar reaches into her purse and pulls out a familiar brand. She sticks the cigarette in her mouth.

"That's so bad for you," I mock.

"Shut up," she says, "If I'm going to die young, you can bet I'm going to live the rest of it very fast."

"Dancing. Stalking. Smoking. All these things were beyond you, Skye. Have to say, I like the new you. What's next?"

She stops. Gray eyes drift upwards to a garish sign. On a whim, she drops the cigarette, and starts toward a line for the roller coaster. Like she won't live long enough to accomplish both.

"Come on, Len!"

I shake my head.

"Don't be a wimp!"

I follow her into line, one bursting with teenagers, disgruntled fathers and their youngsters. A human train moves along at a snail's pace as I shuffle between sides uncomfortably.

"I thought you hated roller coasters," I remark.

"*You* hate roller coasters, Len."

"I take it this is something else you're actively embracing?"

"What can I say? I'm not going to die in a hospital bed, at least."

One of the dads in front of us overhears Skylar and glares back at her.

"Don't worry. I'm not contagious," she clarifies, "Although, it's not really nice to stare at sick people."

The man mutters something and looks away.

I check whether my jaw is still attached to my cheekbones.

"Wow."

"What? Because I told him to mind his own business?" she asks.

"I don't think I've ever seen you so confrontational with strangers."

"I guess a lot does change in a decade."

The line continues to push forward, twelve people at a time. From where we started, it's progressed a little over halfway. The structure to our left shudders with the sounds of rumbling train-cars and their cheering occupants.

"So I think it's my turn to ask a question," I say.

"Shoot."

"If the doctors came to you tomorrow morning and said they'd been wrong; you were going to live for another ten years, the whole shebang. Would it change anything?"

"I'm not sure what you're asking," she says, "Are you asking whether I'd keep doing crazy things I hate just for the sake of doing them, or whether I'd go back to my old life and revert back to who I used to be?"

"That phrasing works."

She thinks on it, as if building the perfect answer in her brain.

"The doctor who came to my room with the MRI results couldn't have been older than twenty-five. I don't think she'd ever had to personally tell a patient anything like that. It took a while to stop beating around the bush and finally tell me. I know what a blood clot is. She only proved healthy people shouldn't hand out death sentences. Their delivery sucks."

""Do you always talk like you're already dead?"

"In a way, I am. I did the denial thing, the anger and bargaining. I got to depression and I slept. A lot. Somewhere, in that huge clusterfuck of recurrent nightmares, there was a bit of serenity. But the doctors aren't wrong, Leonard. Dying changes something in you. Even if they came to me tomorrow and told me they were, it's part of me now. I'll always live today like it's my last."

"I'm sorry," I say, "I didn't mean to upset you."

54

Skylar wraps her fingers around the thick of my wrist.

"You have no reason to be sorry."

How can she be so calm?

Why doesn't her voice waiver, or her eyes tear?

"If anything, Leonard, I have everything to thank you for."

Ten steps to go.

I am not going to enjoy this.

"Why is that ?"

One of the trains comes to rest above us. Footsteps pound across the opposite end of the platform, a crowd spilling down a different staircase. Some are carried off into other corners of the carnival. Others rendezvous with their friends at the back of the line, ranting and raving about how great the ride was and vowing a repeat performance.

I can see the train cars now.

"I don't know," she replies, "With you, there doesn't have to be a *thing.*"

"A *thing?*"

"The thousand pound elephant in the room called death?" she asks. "For the writers among us, let's call it 'dying with dignity'."

"You remembered," I say, somewhat impressed.

She grins. "Of course I do. Leonard the aspiring writer. It was romantic. I loved that about you. But I haven't seen your name much at the bookstore, so I wasn't sure how to broach that topic."

"I wrote a couple. Published none."

"Yeah," she says, "well, don't give up on your dreams, sweetie. Your day job's not doing you any favours."

"Funny. My parents always told me the opposite."

"And how are they?"

"Dead."

"I'm sorry. Natural?"

"Car crash. Nine years ago. And I've made my peace with it. Not sure Luke has, but he has way too many other, self-created problems to deal with first. And that's kind of what I'm trying to say here, Skye."

"About what?"

"Dying with dignity includes your family, too. Now, I'm not going through what you are, and it's not my place, but I would want my family to not....be caught by surprise, you know?"

We're almost at the gate now. The smell of sweat is pervasive and nauseating.

"That's the problem," Skylar says, "Telling the world will make me look vulnerable. I don't want to look vulnerable. Not many choose the timing, but some of us can control the circumstances. I'm not going to be kept alive by machines. *That*, to me, is not dignity."

Another set of cars unloads and finally we're standing at remotely opened gates. The operator sits in a booth to our right. Two college girls ushering people in and out like a revolving door every few minutes compare boyfriends and nail colors in their downtime.

"You ready?" Skylar asks as the next car comes

rolling in and several wheezing people take their leave down the other side.

"Abso-fuckin'-lutely not."

She chuckles, slaps me in the chest with the back of her hand.

"Suck it up, buttercup. I'm forcing you to do this one time. Not only will you live, but I'll have you home to your fiancee by eleven."

The gate opens and we take our seats. The cold steel car locks its occupants in with colder steel bars cranking down in our laps. To make matters worse, there's not much protection on either side of me.

"I'm not going to lie," I say. "I've never been on a roller coaster."

A schoolgirl giggle escapes her lips.

"Double score for me."

Dinner parties.

They serve as another reminder we're getting older and lonelier, but not to worry; bottles of red wine are in abundant supply to help us ease the transition. Appetizers allow us to indulge memories of better days with a side of non-trans fat. Guests bring dishes of main courses and desserts and they bring six-packs as they carry a bitter spouse in tow. For a few hours, we divide the tensions in the room by filling it with fake smiles and polite conversation.

Tonight I have to deal with it. For Claire's sake. Standing in our kitchen, cutting up vegetables, she pretends she's fine. Hair done, sporting a white blouse, black skirt and her fanciest jewelry. I know the mask too well. She's dolled up her anxiety and wrapped it in a neat bow. Claire needs a distraction. The school giving her a week off for the most recent incident is hardly encouragement. It's the excuse she needs to get herself worked up.

So I have a new job; keeping my girlfriend from hitting alert status red.

Luke and Monica are the first to arrive. My brother, dressed in a Slayer t-shirt and jeans, is armed to the teeth with booze. A thick mane is sprouting under his chin and spreading to his cheeks. His lovely wife, on the other hand, is dressed in a black one-piece. Fake diamond rings hang from earlobes, pitch-black hair drawn back in a bun.

"Hi Len," she says, kissing my cheek as I return the gesture. "Looks like neither of you boys know how to dress for social events, as usual."

Monica has always had her way with snippy remarks and little criticisms designed to be planted where she thinks they will hurt. After the first year, I took a cue from Luke and simply ignored her forked tongue.

"If you're referring to the fact I'm not wearing Ralph Lauren, I have to tell you. This is my happy place. What infamous air metal bands wear to social gatherings is the official dress code here."

She rolls her eyes and pushes past me.

I turn to Luke, as Monica joins Claire in the kitchen.

"Are you coming in, or do you want me to bring you dinner when it's ready?"

Luke steps forward and we embrace.

"How are you, brother?" he asks. "Still shooting the shit?"

"Somewhat, but I'd like to know what shit you've been shooting. I like the look. Very you."

We both grin and he steps inside, removing his shoes. I take the beer and arrange it in the fridge on the top shelf. Luke takes a seat on the couch in front of the TV. I leave the girls to themselves, bringing beers to the living room. My brother tunes the channel to hockey playoffs. I hand him one of the Alexander Keith cans he brought and take a seat beside him. I'm not much for sports but even less for girl talk. This seems to be the lesser of two evils.

Pete arrives next. The first thing I always notice about my assistant manager is he makes no attempt whatsoever to tame his hair or hide the atrocity remaining in its place.

A cute twenty-something redhead hangs off his left arm. Her breasts are just about popping out of a one-piece and her face is covered in glitter. Shoulder-length hair is held in place by innumerable bobby-pins.

"Leonard! Good to see you, buddy," he says.

"Pete," I reply, "I see you brought the cavalry."

The girl emits a shy smile.

I extend my hand.

"Hi. I'm Leonard. Whatever this guy says about me, he's just mad because I made him work last weekend."

She takes my hand and shakes it.

"Hi, Leonard. My name is Stephanie."

"Please, guys, come in."

More introductions are made to Stephanie over the next few moments. It's about what I expect. Claire welcomes her with a hug. Monica shakes her hand with a sour expression, holding a glass at shoulder level. Stephanie starts helping in the kitchen, while Pete gravitates to the hockey game. Pittsburgh is in the final running for its second consecutive shot at the Cup against New Jersey. Within moments, both Pete and Luke are yelling at the flat-screen, bottles of beer above their heads.

Rounding out the guests a half hour later- and momentarily saving our ears from Luke cursing at Jersey's offensive- is Renee, Claire's sister. No plus-one, as expected.

These two are twins in every sense of the word, only separated by the fifteen months between them. They grew up together in Orillia, a small city north of Toronto. Both moved down here for university. Both started in Criminology and changed majors in second year. Renee is the same height as Claire, her features a little pudgier and hair dyed dark brown.

Claire has the door this time. I opt to stay in the recliner and keep my mouth shut. Renee and I aren't the best of friends. Unlike my silly feuds with Monica- which I consider a very sarcastic form of entertainment- Renee disapproves of me.

The girls embrace in the doorway.

"Hey honey," Renee says, "I'm so sorry about what happened."

They separate.

"If there's anything I can do, just let me know, okay?"

"Thanks. We'll talk about it later?"

Renee reaches out and touches her arm.

"Of course. Can I do anything to help?"

Claire chuckles.

"Think I have more help than my kitchen can fit."

"Then I'll just join the boys," Renee says.

I try not to participate in the staring contest as she stops in front of me.

"Hey, Leonard."

Jersey scores against Pittsburgh, nine minutes into the second period, sending Luke into a fit of cursing. Pete watches him in disgust for all of a half-second before joining in the obscenities to draw Stephanie out the kitchen. Only the levitating smells of good food come spilling out.

Pete is really not a hockey guy.

Renee turns back to me.

"How are you?" she asks.

"I'm not sure. Is this part of your attempt to be nice to me?"

She shrugs.

"Let's say I've accepted you're a thorn that's not going away."

"Well then," I say, "I guess I've accepted I'm not going away either."

She's only civil because of Claire. A twitch at the corner of her lips, tightened jaw, and the culling of harsh words don't go unnoticed. She takes a seat on the couch and goes about introducing herself to Pete. The second period is coming to an end and the boys are winding down. Luke drains his beer and departs to get another.

When he returns, he taps me on the shoulder.

"Want to join me for a smoke?"

I bolt from the chair.

"Let's go."

At the far end of the living room is a small door which leads to an enclosed balcony. The windows are lazy sheets of screen designed to keep the insects out in summer and bitter Canadian winter winds eight months of the year. They fail on both counts.

Our landlord, Avery, drives a hard bargain.

Two lawn chairs salvaged from Claire's parents are loosely arranged around a small table she bought at the flea market. Otherwise, we've made no attempt to make it any more aesthetically appealing.

"She's being nicer than usual," Luke observes.

"Renee?"

"Mm." He lights a cigarette between his lips with a book of matches. A mixed cloud of burning tobacco and sulfur fills the small space. "Not trying to take your head off, for once."

"Sure seems that way," I reply. "Give me one of those."

"Cigarettes? Thought you quit this shit."

He offers the open pack and I grab one, yanking the cigarette he's puffing from his lips to light mine. Loose ends of paper and tobacco leaves catch above the embers. A harsh cloud pours into my lungs and I cough slightly. It's been seven years since I smoked one. Blue smoke billows from my nostrils.

"So what exactly happened?" Luke asks.

"With Claire?"

"Mm."

I let out a long funnel of blue air.

"Okay, but you didn't hear this from me. The short version goes like this: some second-grade white boy attacked a Muslim kid and nicknamed him terrorist. One of Claire's students."

"Whose was Claire's student?"

"The Muslim kid."

"This happened in Claire's classroom?"

"Do you want to hear the story or not?"

"Why else would I asked?"

"Then shut up and let me tell the story." Long drag on my cigarette. Exhale. "The school board suspended both boys. Claire was pretty shaken by the whole thing. Apparently the trailer park tyke was learning at home it's alright to hit people you think might be linked to Al-Qaeda.

"Anyway, the kids came back yesterday. Stevie used the opportunity to compound his troubles. Brought a knife to school. His teacher saw him playing with it, and tried to confiscate the thing. Stevie sliced her up. Kids panicked; most of them fled the classroom, and Stevie ran off in the confusion."

"Holy shit."

Another drag and the hanging ash splits off the remains of the cigarette, plummeting to the peeling carpet floor.

"The injured teacher was Claire's friend Bonnie. He swiped her in the arm, below the throat and just above the eye. Bonnie hit her head off a desk and got knocked out. One of the students ran next door to Claire. Police were called."

"I imagine she didn't take that too well," Luke quips.

"She was almost despondent when I came to take her home. Real mess. Just fell into bed and wept half the afternoon. Wouldn't eat. Wouldn't speak. When I tried to sit with her, she looked the other way and said nothing."

Luke takes a long swig from his beer can, but struggles to swallow it. He gets it down and obliges retaliatory belching.

"Everything OK, Luke? You look a little haggard."

His eyes scan the room. For what, I'm not sure. Quick solutions, escape routes; a way out of his brain. Left hand massages his right, which happens to be crushing the depleted aluminum cylinder between marathon sips. He finishes one can and starts another.

"Monica thinks I'm fucking around on her," he finally admits.

I sit back in the squeaky, uncomfortable chair, pulling on the last of the cigarette.

"Really?"

Times of truth, Luke doesn't do eye-to-eye.

"She's kind of right."

"*Really?*"

"Thought it was harmless. Not like Valerie. Not like I slept with the broad. I was drinking with the boys from work when we met. She gave me her number after I'd bought her a drink. Sex on the Beach. Fuckin' disgusting but she was hot, you know? I called her a few days later and we had a kind of date."

"A kind of date," I repeat.

"Don't look at me like that, you fucking tool. Monica was in the States for a week with her parents seeing the Grand Canyon. That, and we've been nothing but miserable with each other lately. Fighting over things that draw the line, man. Like, putting the fucking seat down after I take a piss. Who does that, right?"

"God forbid."

"Anyway, this was nice. We went to dinner a couple times. There was a click. Small, but it was a click. I just...realized all the things I miss when the relationship is new and exciting, y'know?"

Do I condone this?

"Len, I've been married for seven years. Eight in September. I'm going crazy, bound to someone who refuses to bear my children. Monica asks twenty fucking questions every time I leave the house. We spend every second together fighting. I say I'll leave her; she shrugs it off, like I'm not able to. I say I love her and she starts yelling at me.

"You know, it was nice to have dinner with someone who doesn't insist we eat in silence. It was nice to look across the table, one fucking time, to somebody with a soul. Take Monica to dinner? Most terrible thing you could imagine. She talks to the waiter more than me."

Luke takes a long, recuperative breath.

"You done?" I ask.

Luke crushes his beer can and chucks it at the wooden wall. It ricochets back onto the floor, and reluctantly settles.

"Yeah," he says.

"Good, because you have to listen to me. This road you're on- it gets pretty rocky. All I'm going to say to you is: all the pussy and college girls in the world are not going to fix the fact you're unhappy with Monica. Come clean, break it off and fix it, or continue, divorce Monica and live with yourself. Those are your only options here."

"I'll think about it, Len. Promise."

The door behind us opens and Claire sticks her head out.

"Dinner, boys. You coming?"

"Yeah," I say, "Want some help?"

"Sure."

I join her in the dark of the doorway. She kisses me. Her face is warm from the kitchen, I tell her she's beautiful and she blushes.

"We'll continue this talk later, okay?" I say to Luke.

Taking Claire's hand, we join the others at makeshift dining area- a folding card table disguised with cherry red tablecloth, although a gold one couldn't hide its tackiness. A giant roast awaits carnivores at the table, and a slew of vegetarian dishes- chickpea salads, pastas and of course, vegetables- await Renee, who has never eaten a steak as long as we've known each other.

Luke joins us a few moments later, full of wisecracks and back to his somewhat normal self.

The girls talk about the wedding and how beautiful Claire will look in her dress. Pete finally takes a hint and backs off Stephanie, who's taken a hint from Monica and turned her chatterbox dial down a few notches. Luke gets more and more drunk; Renee and Claire get more and more drunk, and I listen to slurring of speech and the rocking of bodies while sipping on a soda. By the time dinner finishes, my fiancee and her sister are plastered and dancing around the living room to Michael Jackson and Janis Joplin.

A few minutes in life offer what the rest of them cannot; the opportunity to let go of the world for that period in time, and let it try going on without you. It's a pocket in the stress of planning weddings; a sock in the mouth of angry wives, unsuspecting girlfriends and the natural order of things. The uncorking of wine bottles is synonymous with the sharing of stories and laughter; estrangement is left at the door and we can all conditionally be called friends.

A relationship is like a story. It has settings, plot and characters, supporting actors and is loaded to the brim with conflict. Some of them are page-turners, keeping readers hooked until the very end; others are boring and represent lost interest after a couple chapters. Many don't survive the first paragraph. And even still, some relationships collapse in the middle like a house of cards. Somewhere in the drama and self-deception, novelty wears off and the book just has to be put down.

It could be argued a good relationship never finds its climax, opting to coast forever into branching narratives.

Whatever the case, it's a story requiring the active participation of two authors whose perspectives can peacefully co-exist. When one of the writers checks out, it's hard to keep the plot going without some major mishaps. Like finding out your boyfriend's been doing that cute lady from the bookstore on the side. If he's an even bigger tool, you're engaged to marry him and he's spending time with dying ex-girlfriends behind your back.

This writer has checked out.

Claire and Renee return around noon from their weekend home to Orillia. The apartment is spic and span. I spent the last two hours making it perfect- dishes done, floor mopped and laundry started.

"We got a new microwave!" Claire exclaims. "Hi, honey."

"Hey yourself!"

She walks to where I unabashedly sit, vacantly watching the Cartoon Network with a bowl of popcorn in my lap. Planting a kiss on my lips, she looks at the TV.

"Roadrunner?"

"You know it."

She kisses me again and settles on the couch. I lay my hand around her shoulder, and her head falls to rest on mine.

"Well when you're done watching your cartoons, will you grab the microwave from Renee's car?"

Renee joins us and looks at the TV as well.

"Seriously? How old are you?"

"Twenty-eight."

"Going on?"

"Twenty-nine, I believe."

"Is this why you didn't pick up all weekend?"

"No, actually," I say. "It rained all fucking weekend and because my bosses never listen, the roof caved and we had to close for a day so contractors could come and repair it. I thought about staying open, but personally, I don't care that much at this very moment. Thanks for your concern, though."

"Renee," Claire says, "cool it. I thought we talked about this. You two really need to learn how to be nice to each other." The tone changes as she turns back to me. "How was your weekend, Len? Apart from the store."

"I'm not sure. I would tell you, but you look pretty excited to tell me about yours."

Renee, shaking her head, takes to the recliner. For the next twenty minutes, I hear all about their adventure home. The smell of Mom's kitchen and the amazing food and cousins she hadn't seen in forever came to visit. For the most part, I just listen as Renee stews in her corner, interjecting with slight clarifications about this or that.

I think Claire has gotten over the Incident. School is almost out, and the board will have themselves a summer fighting over variations of long-term strategy for incidents such as these. Tonight she wants to go see her friend Bonnie, who is on indefinite leave of absence.

So much for my cartoons.

Renee stands and says she has to go.

"Len, can you grab the microwave?" Claire asks. "It's in the trunk. Be careful."

I leave the comfort of the couch, placing the popcorn bowl on the kitchen counter. Renee says her goodbyes and gushes about what a wonderful weekend it was; they should do it again soon. She follows my lead out of the apartment. We make it to the stairs without a word, then to the door, and I hope she can keep her mouth shut. Once we are in the parking lot, where her car is haphazardly double-parked, she shatters that hope.

"So why didn't you pick up all weekend?"

I squint one eye in the sunlight.

"Those leggings really suit you, Renee," I say, "I'm sorry. I could resist, initially, but you're really pushing my buttons here."

She opens her trunk.

"It's fine. I know Claire won't hear a word of it. You've just got her wrapped around your little finger. She wants me to leave it alone." She crosses her arms. "Well, take the fucking microwave, already!"

Slow movements, Leonard.

I reach out and grab the boxed appliance, which is surprisingly lightweight.

She slams the trunk door.

"Don't think for a second," Renee says, " I don't know what you're doing, Leonard. And if I find out you're dicking around on her-"

"Renee, I know about Mark."

"-destroy you. I will make your life hell. What did you say?"

Shit. If I remember correctly, she's not supposed to know I know what only Claire should know.

"It's simple to see," I say, "your ex-husband is a lying sack of shit who ditched you for another woman. Not once, but twice now. I get it. The guy's not around to blame, and I used to have a reputation for doing this kind of thing, so let's blame Leonard. Right?"

I take it from her appalled expression I'm somewhere in the range of being correct on this one.

"How dare you?" she says, "That is none of your fucking business."

"It is until you stop making our personal life choices any of yours."

"Sleeping with other people is not her choice. It's a choice you make, and she shouldn't have to pay for it like I did! So watch out, buddy! I got, what? Two weeks until you get married?"

Flattering as it is, I can't afford to have Renee on my tail the whole time.

"And if you find nothing?" I ask.

She shrugs.

"Then I'll forever hold my peace. But if you're fucking around on her, Len, I swear to God your life will become extremely unpleasant. Do you understand me?"

This microwave is getting tired of being held.

"Then I will see you bright and early June sixteenth, yeah?"

She opens the driver's door and climbs in, rolling down the windows. The sweltering wave bouncing around in her car is felt on its outside.

"You're a fucking asshole, you know?"

I smile and wave.

"Have a fantastic day."

I don't think she hears me as she speeds away from the curb, merging with traffic and disappearing around the bend. So much for civility. I turn to unlock the door and it jams.

I hate this stupid thing.

Closing the apartment door behind me, I set the white box on the kitchen counter and go about unpacking it. Our old microwave is a hulking green monstrosity which shakes and shudders every time it turns on. The thing is set to begin emitting radiation any day now. I unplug it from the wall and carefully place it on the floor. I'm not an expert on disposing of biohazardous cooking appliances, but I'm quite skilled in marveling at new ones. It has all the fancy knobs and switches where our old one had buttons that needed a forceful push to get things moving.

"This is quite the technological advance, honey," I say.

Claire vacates the couch and joins me.

"It is, isn't it? Mom said after that time it burned her baby carrots, she was sold on buying us a new one."

"Well," I say, "maybe if she didn't put carrots in our freezer, it wouldn't have been necessary to drop them in the middle of Chernobyl."

"I'm not going to complain. It's better than this piece of junk. You should have Avery look at the freezer, though. It's been acting funny again."

I turn the microwave on. It beeps and blinks with great enthusiasm.

"I'll call him tomorrow," I reply. "Renee seemed in a good mood."

Claire rolls her eyes.

"That girl is so frustrating. I wish she would stop harping on my life choices and start concentrating on hers. I love her and all, but on some subjects, it's just better to leave her in the dark."

My thoughts exactly, darling.

"This weekend for instance," she continues, "I figured you were out with Luke or trying to get some work done. I told her this- I can actually trust you- but this whole thing with Mark's really rubbed her the wrong way, and she starts projecting."

"Oh yeah," I interject, "about Mark..."

"Oh God, Len. You didn't say something, did you?"

"Kind of slipped out. It definitely would have gone better if she'd kept her mouth shut. But that's Renee for you."

Claire exhales.

"What did she say now?"

I place our resident bundle of radioactivity in the empty white box, along with Styrofoam padding and sheets of bubble paper. I have yet to decide where it's going. I tell her about the conversation downstairs.

"It was the only way I could get her to back off, babe. I'm sorry."

"I'll talk to her," Claire replies, "but God knows she's not going to be happy I told you."

Like talking really helps. The absolute last thing I need is another crazy woman tailing me. If Skylar is my yin, Renee is positioning herself as my yang and I can't keep tabs on both of them.

"I have nothing to worry about, right?" she asks. It's enough to distract me from my fascination with this wonderful new technology, to seriously gauge the rhetoric of the question. "You're not sleeping around?"

I beckon her to step into my open arms.

"Come here," I say as she obliges. Her blonde head rests against my shoulders and her light breathing permeates the fabric of my shirt.

"You have nothing to worry about, darling. Renee's hurting now but she'll get better. You'll see. And you and I, we're gonna get married in two weeks. Everything's going to be okay."

She nods her head.

"I love you, Leonard."

I know, Claire.

That's the hardest part.

A few minutes later, my cell phone rings. I retrieve it and check the caller ID.

It's Skylar.

Shit.

I flip the cell phone open.

"Hey."

Silence on the other end. I pull the phone away, checking to make sure I'm actually connected.

"Hello?"

Heavy, labored breathing.

"Skylar?"

Sniveling.

"I need you," she says. "Please come. I'm outside."

"Are you alright?"

Hesitant.

"No."

I close my eyes.

"I'll be right there," I say.

She hangs up.

I approach the car. I told Claire I would only be a few minutes, but she seemed unworried after her weekend adventure.

The door is locked and I knock on the window, looking back at my living room window. The sound of an unlocking car is noticeably absent to my brain. I crouch down, peering through the glass.

Skylar is in the driver's seat, her head pressed against the steering wheel, hair draped around her face. Her shoulder blades are rising and falling inconsistently as she tries to muffle sobs against the twelve o'clock, fingers wrapped around ten and two.

"Skye," I say, "Want to unlock the door?"

Without looking, her hand reaches out, feeling for the automatic locks. With the door open, I climb into the passenger seat. I extend my arms to her, gently prying her grip from the steering wheel and taking her in my arms.

Her arms tighten around my neck and her head falls onto my shoulder. These are not tears of trauma or mere sadness. This is a tsunami washing over desolate beach fronts. Her hands are cold and clammy against the nape of my neck. Her entire body shudders with unimaginable force for such a tiny girl. For a moment she comes within some semblance of control, but it eludes her and she bursts back into tears.

"I don't want to die, Leonard," Skylar says. "Don't let me die."

I can't go back now. I can't abandon her to die alone. I wish I could promise Skylar another ten years but I'm done making empty promises. I wish I could get better answers than ones I'm finding.

I'm not God. I create, destroy and manipulate rules of reality to serve my purposes as a writer. But when the real malevolent forces of the universe come along and render fragile lives meaningless, playing God isn't really great sportsmanship.

As she drives away, I realize I've been coming at this from the wrong angle. If there really exists a one and only God, and we're engaged in some twisted chess match, maybe this is his way of telling me I fail at my chosen craft.

"She's leaving me, man. She's really doing it."

Nobody appreciates their world crashing down on them. To wake up to a Monday morning which plays out like any Monday morning. Putting on breakfast, having a smoke, trying to kiss your sullen wife on the way out the door, only for her to push you aside.

Driving to work, thinking how you wish to be free of the emotional overload. Coming home at five o'clock to get exactly what you wished for. The relief you spent months and even years imagining turns out to be an even bigger bitch than the one you're trying to be rid of.

Relief is a white envelope with your name scrawled across it on top of an empty dresser.

I can't live where our parents raised us. It has fallen into disrepair under my brother's watch, with peeling panels so bad we could easily have inherited Boo Radley's house. Tears inadvertently make their way down Luke's face as he paces between one end of the porch to the other, where Dad used to read us the newspaper, unwilling to school us in fairy tales and classic stories, and Mom served us lemonade on scorching hot days.

"Shit man," he says, "All I can think about now is....fuckin' Valerie."

"Was that meant to be two sentences? Or one?"

He doesn't respond. Between sniveling and incessant pacing, I've gotten two coherent sentences out of him in the ten minutes I've been here. The eight empty beer cans beside his chair could be a factor.

"Look, man," I say, "You and I both know this is a long time coming. How many days have I come over here, and all you could talk about, complain about, was Monica? Look on the bright side here: she can't take the house. Well, she can try, but I'll step up and claim my stake in it. All for you, buddy."

Luke gets some semblance of self-control. He's still pacing, but at this point, I'll take anything as a sign of improvement.

"You think that's what I'm worried about, Len?"

"Well, when you get to divorce proceedings, you'll be glad someone thought of it."

"My wife is fucking around! She said there's someone else!"

"Which is exactly why you should cut your losses now. You two are *always* fucking around on each other. I mean, first there was Carla and then Valerie and this chick you went to dinner with, but didn't tell me her name. What was her name?"

"Rebecca," Luke says, "And I don't even want to think about divorce. First one was bad enough. There's always a lawyer. There's always a fucking clause, always something standing between you and the person you're trying to talk to. Then? She swoops in and starts taking shit. It starts with the VCR. Next thing you know, it's the goddamn china cabinet. Before you know it, she's taken everything and left you with a box-spring and a fucking table knife."

Luke returns to his chair.

"Except it's not going to end that way that, Len. Not this time. I'm not losing another wife. I'm thirty years old. You think I want to go out into the world and try to find a woman who will love me and fold my laundry and cook me food? If I have to stop cheating and start turning broads away, so be it. But I have to win her back."

"I can't tell you how glad I am you sat down,"

"And you're going to help me," he finishes.

My spine slouches in the folding chair.

"Luke, you can't be serious."

His expression fills in gaps of my disbelief.

I don't have the time to chase ghosts. There's work to be done, and with all these little distractions I'll never get there in time. There's no telling whether Renee was serious about watching me, or if it's solely intimidation. Skylar pops up where and when she wants, and now I'm about to be dragged on a goose-chase for a man whose name we don't even know.

I can't turn him away. I won't say no to my brother.

My best hope lies in talking him out of it.

"What makes you think Monica can be convinced to come back? If there's someone else, she obviously feels the relationship no longer works. Maybe you should just accept it. Divorce is coming, whether you like it or not."

"Fuck you," he says, "You may be willing to run away from your problems, Len, but some of us don't just go down without a fight. I know this marriage is worth saving. If you're not willing to step up and help, I'll just do it on my own."

So much for that idea.

"First of all," I say, "take a pill or something. Come down to Earth a little. Once your feet are back on the ground, come up with a plan. If it makes sense, I'll help you. If it's absolutely fucking ridiculous, then I'm going to have to ask you to reconsider just how much Monica means to you. If you're gonna go ape-shit on this guy, let me know in advance, okay? That's really all I ask."

We stand and I hug him.

"I have to go. Claire has this function at her school she wants me to go to. I'll come by tomorrow afternoon and check on you."

I pull away.

"You're not going to do something crazy, are you?" I ask.

Luke shakes his head. I don't really have a function to attend and Claire's likely been called to wherever Monica is staying to perform similar duties. The woman doesn't have many people she calls friends.

I feel bad about leaving him but I have things to do. Like actually keep the store I just closed up to come here, afloat.

"No," Luke says, "nothing crazy."

"Good. I'll see you later."

Turning and walking to the edge of the porch, down the three cracked planks of woods functioning as stairs, I look out into the street. Where the children normally play, a red Toyota Echo is parked at the curb. Where the bikes fall when kids turn their attention to skateboarding and water-guns is Renee, watching me through dark windows. She makes no attempt to appear hidden; her eyes follow me in plain sight.

I approach the car as she rolls down her power windows.

"Renee," I say, "fancy seeing you here. I take it you're looking to buy one of the fine houses this neighborhood has to offer?"

She chews a piece of gum, smacking her lips as the blue ball of rubber bounces between both sides of her mouth. Overdressed for the weather, as always, with a pair of cheap shades atop her head; this woman has little fashion sense.

"Just making sure you are where you say you are."

"I take it you have nothing better to do than be checking up on me."

"Like I said, Leonard. I have only Claire's best interest at heart, and I don't think you are in her best interest. She told you about Mark and...fine. You are supposed to be her confidante, after all. But I know you're up to something. You may have Claire fooled in all the right places, but I'm going to find out where it is you always disappear to. Now, please get your hands off my car before you lose them."

"You really are a special kind of person, aren't you?"

Renee smiles.

"If you're trying to hurt my feelings, you're doing a terrible job," she says.

I lean in closer, just so I'm sure she hears the undertones of my words; just so I'm sure Renee fully understands me.

"Newsflash?"

"Please," she grins, "indulge me."

"You're really starting to get on my fucking nerves. Stop following me or we'll bring Claire into this. And if you're right, that I have her in all the right places, Renee? Then I think your relationship is going to take a serious hit. I don't need your bullshit and neither does Claire. So do us all a favor and back off, will you?"

I back away, removing my hands from the car.

She's still smiling, smacking the gum in her mouth. I know I can't hit her and I know I can't kill her, but she's making my life...uncomfortable. Shining a light in the holes of a wall I'm desperately trying to hold together, hoping a dirty rodent will pop out.

I have to make her go away.

Renee reaches down and puts the car into drive.

"You got it, boss," she says.

"Wait. That's it?"

No snide remarks or dances with rhetoric? It smells a little too easy, if you ask me.

"Maybe I misjudged you, Leonard. At first it seemed you didn't care a whole lot, but I'll give you the benefit of the doubt here. It's not worth alienating Claire over pure speculation, is it? You just might make a good husband after all. Just don't prove me right, or you'll be sorry."

Did that actually work?

"You have a fantastic day," Renee quips before releasing her foot on the brake and speeding away. I'm left walking in the dust of her screeching wheels, not quite patting myself on the back but not quite ready to accept she's stepped aside.

There are too many moving parts. Luke and Monica, Skylar and Renee. There are too many polar opposites; too many yin and too many yang. My plan to prevent a nervous breakdown just jumped from calculated risk to a delicate balancing act and my relationship with Claire is the most fragile object being thrown up into thin air.

Grocery stores. They're a crucial cornerstone of anyone's life. It's a meeting place, a lonely place and everything in between. It's foreshadowing in its most primal form. The shape of meals to come is laid out on freezer racks, in discount baskets and on the shelves of claustrophobic aisles. People dance around each other with plastic shopping carts, all trying to find their way to the special deal on page three of the weekly flyer. The employees in the deli smile and joke with each other while serving ham shavings and turkey breasts to the general public; workers in the produce section whistle to themselves, and every cashier on duty today looks absolutely miserable.

It's yet another place to watch little idiosyncrasies unfold as seeds of conflict are planted over prime cuts and bread baskets. Where one can disappear with the greatest of anonymity into the frozen section, and where sleep-deprived university students come to make the worst dietary choices possible.

There's some first-rate material found here.

"Honey," Claire asks, "do you remember if we're almost out of garlic? I could have sworn we had at least a clove left."

Some people, on the other hand, just tag along to push the shopping cart. My fiancee and I don't share the same passion for crowded places.

"Might want to grab some. Just to be safe," I say, separating a small plastic bag from its perforated roll and filling it with Granny Smith apples. The red ones just don't it for me. "Any idea what you want to do for dinner?"

"Oh, didn't I tell you? I have dinner with Monica. I tried to get out of it but she was pretty persuasive. You're welcome to tag along if you like."

I'd sooner stick my finger in the deli slicer.

"I close tonight, remember?" I say, and the matter is settled.

There is no need to talk about Renee. Every time Claire's forced to play mediator, we just end up in gridlock anyway. I won't really believe she's backed off so easily; It's not Renee's way. I just have to keep my eyes peeled and hope for the best.

My cell phone rings.

Mandy. She's probably wondering why I haven't called her back; I can only assume that was the point of the first ten voicemails I haven't listened to.

Think fast, Leonard.

"It's Daryl," I say, unsure why I feel the need to lie. "I'm gonna take this somewhere quieter, okay? I'll be right back."

I walk away, past neatly arranged depictions of baby carrots, iceberg lettuce and onions, on showcase as they it were in an art gallery. When I've established a distance out of Claire's earshot, I answer the call.

"Hey," I say, "Can't really talk."

"Leonard, don't hang up."

I stop walking.

"What's wrong, Mandy? You're not calling from the store."

"Nothing! I mean, something's up but I wouldn't say it's wrong."

"Stop calling me. Please, unless it's work related."

"Fine. It's work related."

"Alright," I say, "but make it quick."

"I want us to be together, Leonard. Don't get married."

This takes a moment to register. It's weight my eyelids can't bear and they momentarily blanket sight. In the brief absence of reality, my brain is at the ready to explode.

"What do you want me to do?" she asks.

"Nothing," I reply. "Stop calling me, Mandy."

I hang up and return to Claire, who's murmuring the lyrics to "Hungry Heart" by Springsteen in the soup aisle.

"Hey," she says, "how's Daryl doing?"

On your feet, Leonard.

"As long as I come within ten percent of budget, he's got nothing. Can yell and grovel all he wants."

"You're such a good employee. They're lucky to have you. So am I." she says.

She plants a kiss on my lips and returns to deciding between the premium brand of mushroom soup and the knockoff. I have more important matters to contemplate than lunch in a can.

Sometimes it scares me how good a liar I am.

Luke hasn't moved from yesterday. Although the weather is nicer now, with the humid sun setting on the skyline, I could swear he is wearing the same shirt I left him in.

"Am I ever glad to see you," he calls over the porch railing, which provides ample balance for the booze on his breath. "I've been awake all night. Think I found the fucker sticking his tool in Monica. Made some calls and I got a hold of a bartender named Blake Shaughnessy."

I climb the rickety steps, assuming a seat in my usual chair.

"And why do I care about some bartender, exactly?" I ask.

"This guy knows who Monica is, and what rock she's been hiding under. She's been hanging around some big-shot corporate fuck named Georgie Kane."

"Hell of a name."

"Blake doesn't know much about him, but he said Kane does tend to drop in weekdays after work. Blake remembers this tool getting pretty fucking friendly with her."

"So," I conclude, "your solution to your wife leaving you is to call every bar in a three-block radius and twist their employees' arms to give you the dirt on Monica?"

"Exactly," Luke says. "Genius, no?"

"And how do you know they're not pulling your chain?"

"Leonard, you're not hearing me. This fuckwad is boning Monica. Remember her? Short black hair, cranky Monica? My wife?"

"Dresses like a prostitute?"

"That's just low. Are you going to help me or are you gonna keep playing hard to get?"

This is crazy. I suppose his is a natural reaction, though. I know this is important to him and I would never hear the end of it if I refused to help. Still, on top of trying to keep a tandem leash on Skylar, Renee and Claire, my tower of leaning blocks is beginning to look a lot like Pisa.

"What are you going to do when you find this guy?" I ask.

"I'm not sure. I'm kind of flying by the seat of my fucking pants here."

Don't worry, Luke. You're not the only one.

I've been steered off-course by Luke's version of marital Hell. Sitting in his musty cable repair van, parked in the lot of a seedy downtown bar, is not my idea of progress.

At least it's an alibi.

"You do realize we're blatantly obvious, just sitting here?" I ask.

Luke, with a disintegrating cigarette between his fingers, stares at the bar patio. This is not a place where the college kids come or people with self-respect loiter on a Tuesday night.

"Luke?"

"I want him to see me," my brother replies, "That's the first step."

"And what's the second?"

Luke shakes his head.

"I'll know once the first step happens, hopefully." He winces. "God, I wish it hadn't come to this. I wish I could keep my dick in my pants. I wish my marriage wasn't a heap of shit, or Monica wasn't Monica. Then again, I also wish for a hot tub and a Porsche. But I fucking love her, Len. Even with all the ass walking around this city, I happen to be crazy about the one chick with a hard-on for sucking the life out of me. That's gotta be a fucking paradox, right?"

I say nothing.

"For so long, I couldn't wait to be rid of her. We settled into this routine, this comfort zone of lying to each other; lying to ourselves. It was perfectly acceptable to turn out the lights at the end of the day and go to sleep instead of just being honest with each other. She would turn her head the other way, which made me want to do the same. I'd always be jacking off into the wind with Monica, always thinking of some other woman. We'd go for months without sex. I was getting mine on the side so I didn't blow it out of proportion, but none of it was ever as good.

"I've contemplated everything. Maybe I need to see someone. Sex rehab, or whatever the fuck they call it. A doctor of some kind. I've toyed with suicide but I'm not an idiot. I've thought of depression meds or electroshock therapy; anything that will make my brain accept fidelity as a fucking solution."

"I don't believe they go around these days, just randomly shocking people. You could always stick a fork in the socket if you're so eager to try it."

My wisecracking brother is gone; he shrugs off my comments and continues sucking on the end of his cigarette filter. When that one's up, he tosses it through the crack in his window and lights another.

Chain-smoking has a distinct smell, and it's giving me a headache.

"For all that time I spent thinking of my life without her, Len; now all I can think of is the opposite. I don't want to spend the rest of my life filling my bed with other random women. I don't want the Carlas and the Valeries. I don't want the cute redheads or the big-breasted bimbos who trade me dinner for a fucking blow-job. I have to win her back."

I just want this to be over. The lies and the sneaking around are taking their dastardly toll, and Luke's lying and sneaking around are only rubbing it in. My stomach growls and left eyelid twitches with restlessness and my head is in another solar system altogether.

"Okay," I say, "are we going to do this, or what?"

I open my creaky passenger door, which makes the entire vehicle shudder, hoping Luke will follow suit. His fingers reach for the handle and he pushes his door open, climbing out. Not bothering to lock up, he takes lead into the bar.

The place is dark. It smells like old bread and urinals. The walls are painted a horrid yellow, which is appropriate considering the color of its patrons' skin. Several tired sets of eyes look up at us, and I immediately feel uncomfortable at the perfected stillness.

Why the hell would a corporate hot-shot named Georgie Kane associate himself with such venues? He should be on the corner of Delta and Bay with all the Irish pubs and university girls in miniskirts. He should arrive with groups of mid-thirty something suit n' ties who are all passing themselves off as twenty-fives.

The bartender is in his forties, with a thick chinstrap and balding crown. He's dressed in a black shirt and red tie, and watches us as we approach where he stands idle by a cash register.

"Gentlemen," he says, "what will it be?"

Luke removes a twenty-dollar bill from his pocket and slaps it down on the counter.

"You Blake?"

"That's me. You must be the guy who called about your wife."

"*C'est moi, mon ami*," Luke says, "I want to get drunk and have us a conversation, Blake. So pour you a beer, pour me a beer and let's have a chat. If Leonard wants a beer, he can fuckin' have one too."

"I'm good," I say, "Just here for the scenery."

"And you keep the change," my brother concludes. "What'll it be, Blake?"

"Sorry. Can't drink on the job."

"But you can have a conversation and a fucking cola, right?"

"If the price is right. I don't work for free, you know."

Luke produces another twenty and pushes them both in front of the bartender. He looks down at them, takes them in his hand and examines them to make sure they're real.

"Sorry. We get a lot of counterfeits in here. You understand." Blake lowers the bill. "What do you want to know?"

"First things first. What do you have on tap?"

"Canadian, Rickard's and Rickard's Red. I also have Labatt, Stella Artois and Heineken in bottles. Guinness in cans."

"I'll have a Heineken," Luke replies. Blake's head disappears under the cedar oak bar-top and emerges with a green bottle he cracks open and hands to my brother. "Sure you don't want anything, Len?"

I shake my head.

Luke turns back to the bartender.

"How often does this guy come around?"

"Kane?" Blake says, "He's here four nights a week. Comes in with a bunch of his friends around ten. Usually they bring girls, but sometimes it's just them. They're loud and obnoxious and like to start fights, but I'm not going to complain with the cash they bring in, and they don't smell half as bad as some of the poor saps who come waltzing in off the street. So it's a give-and-take."

I have to ask again why Kane and his buddies choose such a dismal location, only this time out loud.

"Because," Blake says, "Georgie's half-brother is the owner of this bar; my boss. Basically? We got space in the back, and Kane likes to entertain the fish he catches. Picks them at the high-end pubs, and brings them here so his young wife won't come home to an awkward situation in their bedroom."

It's a dishonest world out there.

"Did you see if my wife ever went back there with him?" Luke asks.

The bartender grimaces.

"I'm here seven nights a week. Our other bartender quit, and I have a wife with a baby on the way, so I need all the money I can get. I don't think I've ever seen a girl who hasn't been taken back there."

Luke's face turns beet red.

"What does this prick look like?"

"Well, he's tall. Dresses fancy. Slicked hair, always combing it. You could pick him out of a crowd, easy."

"Do you expect him tonight?" Luke asks.

"It's Tuesday. Kane likes Tuesdays. So, probably."

The door behind us opens on cue. A small group of men with short, parted hair and expensive suits walk in. Two girls are with them, maintaining a delicate balance with their high heels. Both hang off the arm of a suit n' tie.

I immediately know which is Georgie Kane. Apparently, Luke sees him too, because his face goes from tomato red to its rotten counterpart.

Kane's taller than the rest of his friends. With a full head of slicked hair and a thick scent of arrogance, he leads the pack with a girl ten years his junior at his side. We lock eyes for a moment before Kane dismisses me. The shoes are more reflective than some mirrors, and as the group takes a seat, he removes his blazer to reveal a perfectly ironed shirt. Not the slightest crease.

Kane takes his seat, back to us.

I can already see where this is going.

"Luke," I say, "don't."

Too late. My brother clears the bar-top and starts walking towards them. I should be stopping him, pulling him out of this place.

Luke stops beside the table.

"Are you Kane?" he asks.

Kane looks up with an expression which can only be described as hubris.

"Do we know each other?"

Without warning, Luke cocks his fist and slams it into the hinges of Kane's jaw. The chair topples with his weight and Kane falls into the lap of his mistress. Luke pulls his fist back as three other guys jump out of their seats, ready to defend their friend and eager for any fight.

Kane rubs his jaw.

Jumping off the bar stool and getting a grip on Luke's arms, I try to pull him away from getting torn to pieces, but he resists and revolts against me.

Blake is about five seconds from calling the cops.

"Luke, come on!" I say.

My brother fights against my grip and naturally, I lose my hold on him. He lunges forward into them, and lands another punch. One of Kane's buddies goes down as another pelts Luke in the face. I reach out and grab his arm. Dragging him to his feet, I heave and pull him past chairs and tables his feet are kicking over and to the door.

"Stay away from my wife!" he yells as I tug at his arm. "I'll fucking kill you, Kane!"

"Luke, come on!"

My brother thrashes against me, and for all my effort, I barely manage to reroute him outside. With Luke cursing and growling like a rabid animal, I can only hope he's not going to bite *my* head off. The night breeze does little to minimize beads of sweat pouring down my cheeks or the dampening of my hair.

"What the fuck was that, man?" I yell as I let go of him; his arm jerks away as if I've pricked him with twenty-five needles. "Didn't I tell you to fucking warn me if you were gonna go absolutely fucking-"

Luke struggles to catch his breath as he cuts me off.

"Don't even fucking start with me, okay?"

The bar door behind us opens and three of Kane's friends waltz out; teeth bared, muscles flexed, shirts untucked, parted hair amiss. It's actually quite hard to tell the difference between them.

I dub them Rob, Bob and Tom.

Kane comes dashing out the door, his face beet-red and Blake in tow. The pacifist bartender is along for the ride to make sure this scuffle shimmies off his property, but Kane is unconcerned with such petty matters. He comes at Luke carrying the spirit of vengeance; his eyes alight to let the world know nobody fucks with Georgie Kane.

"Luke," I say, "we have to go now!"

My brother has the exact same look in his eyes.

If there's anything he loves more than hockey on a high-definition television twice his size, it's a bar fight.

Kane spits on the ground beside him.

Blake lights a cigarette.

The girls arrive outside, fumbling purses and lighters. One of them cheers on Kane as she lights her cancer stick. The brunette whispers to the one I've affectionately labeled Tom.

"Now," Kane says, "I don't know who the fuck you think are, buddy, but we're gonna settle this *mano a mano*. You come into my brother's bar and you start shit before we even exchange names? You made a giant mistake, my friend."

Luke smirks.

"Just stop talking and come at me, bitch."

Kane swings at him with no reservations. Luke ducks the fist and counters, slamming an elbow into Kane's nose. There's a loud pop and he stumbles back, and my brother strikes again. The full force of Luke's knuckles intersect with his opponent's jaw and Kane is launched sideways into the pavement.

At this point Tom stops flirting with the brunette and steps forward as his two buddies rush Luke, only he comes for me.

Tom, in his high-end suit and fancy shoes, looks to be a poor opponent at best. Before he can land a punch, I grab him by the shirt and use my own momentum to slam him into the building's wall. He retaliates, landing a strike between my eyes, but the force of it is weakened.

I let go, clutching my forehead, trying to re-orient. I shut and open my eyes to lose the blur, to no avail.

Tom kicks out and his loafers connect with my cheekbone. The echoing agony rippling through my skull supersedes whatever scrapes and bruises I receive from hitting the ground. In parallel vision, I catch glimpses of exchanged blows, and hear the silhouettes of cussing, but my brain can't process them.

"Len? Len, get up! We have to get out of here!"

Am I dead?

"Len, the cops will be here any second! We have to jet. C'mon, buddy."

I blacked out.

Involuntary muscle movements.

Did he take them all down?

My head is fucking pounding. The heels of my shoes drag across pavement. The opening of a van door and great strain on Luke's part help me into the passenger seat. It feels like half my face's skin has been chiseled off. My eyes are rolling around uselessly in their sockets. It's like staring up at the world from underwater, and pieces of my brain are drowning; primarily, the ones that make visual sense of my nonsensical life.

By the time we reach the second set of lights from the bar, I'm coherent again. Luke, on the other hand, gloats in the midst of his endorphin high.

"Well I feel amazing," he says, "How about you?"

Like I had an intimate encounter with sandpaper.

"Keep it in your pants," I reply, "and tell me I don't look like a steamroller took a liking to me. Did you really lay all those guys to waste?"

He studies my face and chuckles.

"Yeah...for a bunch of dudes passing themselves off as tough guys, they were a bunch of pansies." He studies my face. "Holy mother of mercy fucks, Leonard. You took quite the ass-kicking, didn't you?"

I say nothing.

The light turns green and Luke removes his foot from the brake. His little van moves forward, criss-crossing yellow lines, tram car tracks and poorly designed left turns to get us home. Even this late at night, when paid parking spots are impeded by police cruisers and sidewalks are mobbed with pedestrians, Toronto is alive and bustling.

As he pulls into the cubical slot where his cable van sleeps at night, Luke asks the mother of unforgivable questions.

"What the hell are you going to tell Claire about this?"

This is the first time in weeks I'm not constantly worrying about something, but come to think of it, even that worries me now.

I have a loud ringing in my head and her name is Skylar Bates.

"Okay then. Never mind," he says, "Look, I know you didn't agree with this. I can even admit it was juvenile and stupid. There are bones in my hand that might be broken, and I can't even tell you what they're fucking called. Either way, it means a lot to me, Leonard. Thank you."

"You're welcome," I reply, "but looking back on my part, I think if I was in your position with Claire, I might have done the same thing."

I pause, and before I know it, the words are rolling off my tongue.

"I almost shot a man once to protect a girl. I know it's not the same thing, but it's amazing what lengths you'll go to for someone you love. This guy...well, his name was Desmond Wright, and he was a fucking animal. Used to stand on a corner all day outside her building, against a chain link fence, and deal shit like LSD and heroin to junkies and high school kids. Anyway, he got really friendly with this girl- Eden- for a time, and started fronting her on occasion. But there was this one time she didn't pay him back.

"Wright went and fetched some of his friends, and they started harassing her. She didn't have the money so they demanded sex- yes, even Wright. And when they were done...gang banging her, she still owed on those debts, so they would come back and do it again."

My eyes are burning. I don't know if it's my bruised face or tears coming on, but my voice wavers with it, so I have to assume the latter.

Luke says nothing as I talk.

"The first reaction I had was to leave her. She'd been going downhill for over a year, always taking me with her. She kept it secret from me for months. One day, when she was really upset, I wrangled an entire confession from her. It was one more bomb on top of Mom and Dad, and I lost it. I went to Wright's corner, but he wasn't there. So I waited for him, and when he showed up, I gave him a beating unlike any he'd ever gotten. It felt... primal, like starvation; like it was necessary for me to go on with my life.

"A couple months later, Wright and his boys came to see me. Pinned me against a wall, beat me up some, and held a fucking gun to my head. They put it in my mouth, and Wright said I should remember this image for the rest of my life. He said, 'You should remember it because you're going to wish it had been this quick'. I went home to Eden's apartment, fished a gun out of her sock drawer, and that's when I found the note. The note that said she was leaving me."

Luke reaches into his pocket and retrieves a cigarette he fits between his lips.

"Why have I never heard this story, Len?"

"Because I've never told it to you," I say, "Because I've never told it to anyone. That note was all that stopped me from killing Wright, and thereby saved me life in prison. All I could think about for years afterward was that one day. Every time I heard her name, I thought of the day I was ready to actually kill someone."

"And what do you think of when you say her name now?"

Indexed and filed, with serial numbers in the cabinets of my brain; complete with passwords, biometrics and deadbolts where Eden belongs; where they all belong.

Where Skylar was, and will never return.

"Nothing," I say, "because it's the past now."

We exit the van and say our goodbyes, and my brother embraces me. For once, I am not thinking of what I'm going to tell Claire. As I walk away from the porch of Luke's newly-minted bachelor pad, I can breathe a sigh of relief. For the first time in almost three weeks, I don't have to lie about where I was tonight. I don't need an alibi or a place and time or a restaurant bill. I can tell Claire the truth about something.

Finally.

"What happened to your face?"

The answer to this question is a better story with each telling. Claire, Renee, my bosses, the girl at Starbucks. By the time I get to Veronica, it's the polished turd of a piss-poor adventure that should never be released into the wild, so I substitute a classic.

"The first rule of Fight Club is you don't talk about Fight Club," I reply.

"Funny," she says from behind the counter, filing returns into alphabetical order. The new piercing above her lip has started to swell. "Haven't seen Mandy lately, have you?"

I set about merchandising the concession rack by the cash. My employees are useless.

"They know this is supposed to be straightened before they leave," I mutter. "And no, I haven't. She was a no-show both days this weekend. Once more and she's out of a job."

"Think it has anything to do with you rejecting her ass?"

"How do you know about that?"

Veronica chuckles. "Oh, Leonard. Even bitches who hate each other talk. Of course, I find it amusing, since this place is boring as eff."

"Eff?"

She sighs, lazily shuffling the DVD cases without looking at them. "Jaden is in a copycat phase. Have to curb swearing like a fucking sailor."

Of course Mandy is out there, spreading gossip where I least need it. Unfortunately, she is the least of my concerns. Renee has stopped following me everywhere, but she finds any reason to call or come over. Skylar is sending midnight texts, which I struggle to keep from Claire's innocent handling of my phone; and my bosses are threatening a review for too much missed work.

My head hasn't been here lately.

The threatening cloud cover over Lake Ontario finally gives way to downpour, coating the streets in a darker shade of paint. Traffic up and down the grid has slowed to a crawl. This is one of those days I'm glad I've never owned a car. Besides, I think as I pass wave after wave of people stuck behind red lights or bad drivers; walking builds character. It opens blood flow to the legs and stokes the imagination.

Her apartment building on Murray Street is a half hour on foot. Five minutes after I've stepped out into the rain, passive-aggressive water droplets soak my shirt and pants. With hair matted to my forehead, I stick to the inside of the sidewalk, squeezing through a crowd armed to the teeth with umbrellas of a million shapes and sizes. Horns honk and cabbies shake their fists at crossing pedestrians.

Skylar's building is old and decrepit. It's badly maintained from the outset, with lights that don't work over the doors and a broken buzzer. The grass is brown and the hallway windows are filthy on the outside. Because she can't ring me in, I dial her phone number.

It rings once. Twice. Three times.

On the fourth ring, she picks up.

"I'm outside," I say, "Want to let me in?"

When the door opens a few moments later, it's not the same girl who broke my fear of roller coasters. Skylar appears deathly ill, and light mascara is smeared around her eyes. With pale skin and loosely fitting clothes, even her blonde has lost some color. I follow her down the darkest hallway I've ever occupied into her apartment.

The walls are a light purple and smell like fresh paint-thinner. Floors are unswept, dishes not done. The TV is blaring infomercials by the window in front of a couch complemented by Skylar's outline.

"Sorry about the mess," she says, "It's been a bad couple days."

"Is everything okay?" I ask, shutting the front door behind me. "Where's your sister?"

"Part of the reason it's been a bad couple days. Would you like something to drink? I have water, milk and....water."

"Water is fine, thanks," I say.

Skylar walks to the open concept kitchen at the far end of the apartment and grabs a glass from the overhead cabinet. She runs the tap and returns to me with a tall serving of clear fluid.

"What happened to your face?" she asks.

I take the glass from her shaking hands.

"Got into a fight. You don't look so good yourself, Skye."

"Yeah," she says, "might have something to do with the fact my number is almost up."

She can't even keep her eyes open and she's getting snippy. This could be a bad sign.

"Maybe we should sit down?" I ask.

Skylar nods and I help her toward the couch. It takes her some effort to seat herself, and she winces as she falls back into the cushions. I place the glass of water on the same coffee table she hoists her legs onto. The liquid bounces around the glass as she fidgets, trying to get comfortable.

I take a seat beside her.

"Is there anything you want to tell me?"

Skylar shakes her head.

"Such as?"

"Well, I don't know, Skye. You just disappeared all of a sudden. You look like hell. I thought you would at least return my calls or give me some idea what's going on. Did I do something or say something? You can talk to me, you know."

"Ever think," she says, "not everything is about you, Leonard?"

"What?"

"I mean, did you ever think I might be having a hard time, too? I don't enjoy feeling this way or...living this way?

Where is this coming from?

"I don't understand," I say, "You came to me, Skylar. Not the other way around."

Her cheeks flush and her eyes are red and her lips quiver, but none of these things tell me what's really going inside her head. The crinkles in her forehead don't tell me anything more than do the bullet points of her words.

"I don't know! I don't know anymore!" She takes a moment to recuperate. "I knew doing this wouldn't change the facts. I knew it wouldn't keep me alive any longer. I've already accepted the fact I don't have much time left. But...I thought it would bring me *something*! Anything at all. Even if it meant letting you risk everything- your marriage, your freedom, your sanity- I thought I would reap one last moment of happiness. A sense of closure. But I have nothing."

She rolls her eyes.

"I wanted you to be there, to end it, if no one else would."

"You what?"

"I know. It is a horribly unfair thing to ask of you. I always thought, if I ever saw you again, you would be the exact same person. Deceitful, conniving- I had a million names for you. Leonard the Liar was a favorite. It didn't stop me from playing it out in my head endlessly. What I would say or how I would feel?" She shrugs. "Obviously, you always know what to say, always have the right words and that's what I love about you. You're too gifted for your own good, Leonard."

I think of my father, clinging to life, gasping for air. Fighting for something. If I could have- if he had asked me to end the suffering- I would have pushed past doctors and nurses and smothered him, pulled the plug. Anything.

Is this any different?

"You're right. This is a lot to ask."

She wipes the tears from her eyes.

"It's already taken care of, Leonard. Rather, it will be soon."

"Skye," I say, "do you realize how ridiculous this all sounds?"

112

"That's right. It sounds ridiculous, Leonard, because it is. Because the fact you could truly care about anyone but yourself is fucking ridiculous. Go ahead. Tell me I'm wrong.

"I came home. I paced and I cried and I laughed hysterically when I couldn't cry anymore. Curled up in a ball right there on the floor. Tore at my hair, forced myself to puke up everything I ate and then I just stopped eating. I figured: what's the point? The more and more I chased after something to go on for, the less I came up with."

My God. She tried to kill herself. Looking down at her wrists, now I see the carefully concealed cuts down her forearm in a vertical line, poking out of her sleeve. Shock is overturned by the fury rising in my chest.

Anger is bubbling to the surface and I can't contain the monster in me, pushing upward and outward. She didn't find me so we could reconnect. She found me so I could be her tool. She came into my life with the worst possible timing for her own selfish gains.

"To hell with this," I say.

"What?"

"Do you honestly expect I will kill you? That I'm able to live with myself after doing that, Skye? I'm constantly trying to answer questions I don't have good explanations for. I have my own problems, too!"

Skylar can't even meet my gaze, nor does she want to.

"Now, my future sister-in-law is determined to find out who *you* are, or where I've been disappearing to. Whatever."

"Have you considered telling the truth, Len? It's what most decent people would do."

"You know what, Skylar?" I say, "Fuck you. If you hadn't been stalking me out of your obsession, I would have never needed to consider it! If you hadn't shown up, I would be content in my bliss right now. Life's not perfect, okay, but this is turning into a shitshow now."

"You wouldn't be happy!" she says, "If not through me, you would found another way to fuck up your life and everyone's life who fucking revolves around you, Leonard!

"I honestly believed you when you said you were different. I thought if the man who doesn't believe people are capable of change had done it, maybe it was possible. Guess I'm finally realizing you're the same jerk you've always been, just in a different disguise. You're still the same guy who drove me away."

Unbelievable.

The absolute last thing I need is a lecture from someone who will be dead in less than a week, if she continues down her current path.

Then again, she could be dead in a week regardless.

Skylar calls my name as I walk to the door and reach for the handle. Her cries for my return follow me down the hallway and out the door, into the warm night that has slowed to a drizzle. Water lands on my bare arms and down my scalp; as I lay my eyes upon the darkened pavement of this sparsely occupied road, I don't know whether to laugh or cry. I don't know whether to yell or destroy. Whether to walk on or stand here forever in my pool of rage and diluted understanding.

This is your future, Leonard.

Standing on the cusp of losing everything?

Chasing the foreshadow of my undoing?

Was Renee right about me?

This is your future. This is who you are.

Stepping down to the street, where my shoes seem to be guiding me in a direction all their own, it's time to set the record straight and put my past to bed.

Despite the meager consolation, I walk forward with a sense of impending dread and don't even notice it feels like a pair of eyes are watching me. In the wide net of loneliness being cast over me, I completely fail to notice the red Toyota Echo parked down the street. With the sound of a billion preoccupations playing on repeat in my head, the sound of a car engine coming to life doesn't register, nor do I care enough to listen for it.

The fabric of time is said to heal all wounds. I think that's bullshit. Instead of healing the scars of old, it just piles new ones on top of the older. Time has never been anything but an additional burden. The death of my Mom and Dad left its own depraved effect on me I've never fully processed.

Locking the door to the video store, facing an endless boulevard of pedestrian foot traffic and nightmare parking, the full moon pours over the sidewalk where I fumble with a rusty gate. Nassim and Kyle departed moments earlier, both blasting music in their ears, although Kyle had the earbuds in all night.

It's all in the routine.

"Leonard?"

Jesus. The girl's voice startles me, and the store keys fall. Shit. I only have seconds more to arm this thing. Who would sneak up on me like that?

Mandy, with her black bowl cut and a light blue jacket, must realize the severity of her disturbance, because she backs away.

"Stupid gate," I curse.

"I didn't mean to scare you. Should have seen yourself. Jumped right out of your skin."

I jam the door closed, pushing my body weight. Fuck it. If the store gets broken into, insurance won't cover the losses since the gate is unsecured, but I don't need a midnight visit from contract mall cops.

Click. The key turns in place.

Backing away from the door, I should be stopping to think this through, but I'm done thinking.

116

Being careful and methodical has brought me nothing but misery.

"What you want, Mandy? I'm not giving your job back. Chris signed off on the paperwork yesterday."

She grabs my arm.

"I don't want the job. I want you."

I look down at her fingers, wrapped around my bicep. Firmly, I pull her clasp on it away, holding onto her wrist.

"I don't know how many more ways I can explain this. I don't want you. I have never even wanted you, not even in the back of your dad's station wagon. There's ten years between us, woman, and I'm getting married in a week!."

"Leonard, you're hurting me!"

"Then stop whatever this charade is. Go find a nice boy your own age, Mandy."

A patrol cop emerges from the twenty-four hour store two doors down, sipping coffee from the dome lid that barely seems held on.

I release her, lest he might intervene. As if she sees what I am seeing, she smiles.

"Oh Leonard," Mandy says, "Big mistake."

It's too late. The cop, a younger lad both taller and stronger than I am, has already noticed us. His hair is cropped, with a hint of too much gel.

He approaches us, coffee in one hand, the other outstretched.

"Is there a problem here, ma'am?" he asks Mandy, whose shit-eating grin has dolled up into a fearful arrangement of carefully positioned muscles.

Fuck. Fuck. Fuck.

"Yes officer," she says, "This man assaulted me when I was underage, last year. He refuses to leave me alone."

"What?" I exclaim, "You know that's a lie, *Amanda*. Officer, look…"

The cop lets his coffee cup drop onto the sidewalk. Brown sludge, the premiere brand of corner store grinds, seeps between the eroded cracks. He unholsters a set of handcuffs.

"Please," Mandy pleads, "Officer, I'm tired of fearing for my safety."

The world filters every sound- the revolutions per minute of speeding cars, indistinguishable chatter from passersby and an ambulance wailing in the distance-into a wind tunnel. I hear none of it as the handcuffs fasten both hands behind my waist.

Don't overreact, Leonard.

When my eyes drift up to the street again, that resolution dies a quick and violent death. A familiar face awaits, staring at me from the driver's seat of a very familiar car.

Renee.

Fuck. Fuck. Fuck.

It's midnight. They took my watch, along with the rest of my personal belongings, escorting me into a holding cell with nine other men. In a caged box of battery assault, robbery and a thin guy who won't stop twitching and cursing, I've been reduced to a petty criminal. Even without the familiar, ticking plastic device around my wrist, the habitual time-checker in me keeps glaring at the wall.

The cell is almost the size of my entire living room. Several worn benches run down the middle of this cage. For a Friday night, ten guys sounds too few, but it's early yet.

"What you in for?"

I look behind me.

A stocky, mid-forties gentleman- with rose-colored glasses and thinning hair that's still long enough to dance on his neck- sits upright with arms crossed and a lopsided smile on one of the benches. A thick goatee is strapped to his chin, which is fitting, given the blue Hawaiian shirt and black jeans.

He uncrosses his arms and shuffles to the end of the bench, extending his hand.

"Aaron Calloway. Pleased to meet ya. Me? In because some five-oh thinks I torched a cop car."

I shake his hand.

"And did you?" I ask.

We break it off. Short and sweet.

"Nah," he replies, "I only parked it in a place I knew it would get torched. Finch Avenue. You'd not believe what the saps over there would do to a cruiser."

He stops to pay a moment's attention to the Haitian guy's twitch moving into hyper-drive. "Name's Wallace. I don't know if I believe it's his real name, but the closest he can get to telling me is saying *walla*. I put the rest together myself."

"Sounds more like he needs a doctor."

Calloway laughs.

"You're a funny one, kid. What's your name?"

I look back at the clock. Twelve-oh-five. I called Claire an hour ago. Instead of ensuring I will get out of this place, and assume damage control by getting in touch with my lawyer or Luke; all I could think of was getting to her before Renee does. My thoughts are in panic, my heart has sunken to my stomach's level and I can't help feeling like the stars are aligning against me.

I didn't come here to make friends.

"It doesn't matter what my name is."

"Gonna play like it like that, huh?" Calloway says, "Cool, dude. You had a bad night. I understand . But you look like you're carrying some major bullshit around with you. You and Wallace could have a competition of sorts, if you like. I'm sure your problems can't be worse than his. Just look at the poor bastard." He chuckles at the sight of Wallace's facial tick. "My eighty-year old mother has more control over her motor functions."

Who the hell is this guy?

"You sound like a smart man," I say, "so what are you doing stealing cop cars?"

Another laugh. Slightly creepier, less jolly.

"I'm fucking with you. Drunk and disorderly. Some guy took a stab at my mother's honor, and I taught him some respect." He scoffs. "Like I would steal a fucking cop car. Nah, man. Drunk and disorderly. Assault, maybe. Me? I got a good lawyer. He'll sort this out."

Great. This guy is a creep and a compulsive liar.

"You waiting for something?" Calloway asks.

"What?"

"I said, you look like the kind of guy who's waiting for something bad to happen."

I sigh, peering through the ancient bars which have seen bar brawlers, cop car thieves, drunks and people who got caught up at the wrong place, in the wrong time. They have held the killers and the scum who have passed through these halls. People like Wallace, the Harley Davidson enthusiast in the corner, and people like myself.

This is karma, or something.

"I don't know what's happening," I say, "One day I just woke up and my life was everything I wanted it to be. I had someone who loved me for exactly what I am and I just couldn't fucking deal with it. Now it's just....like I'm living in flashes."

"That's heavy, man."

I don't know why my most intimate thoughts are pouring out to a complete stranger. I guess it's the same principle as a confession, only Calloway and I are trapped on the same side of the box.

"For the first time in my life...for once, I wasn't trying to fill a great, gaping hole. But something in me, some penchant for taking something beautiful and lighting it on fire, to make it something more beautiful-"

"So you fucked up something good," Calloway says, "I've fucked up plenty in my life. I'm fuckin' Irish. People 'been walking all over me since the day I was born. I drink too much and I got three kids, none of whom want anything to do with me. You know why? Because I spent their entire lives walking all over them. Their mothers, too. I pissed away three marriages over a bottle which never lasts more than a fuckin' night. I can't apologize to a single one of them without someone suggesting rehabilitation. So believe me, my friend, we all fuck our good shit up."

The biker, who drives the very definition of masculinity and macho-isms, speaks up.

"True bud," he says, "My old lady booted me. She's a tough cookie but we men have a way of taking a good idea and asking our dicks what they think about it. And the dick only has one answer to anything."

The other men nod in sullied agreement.

Now there's an analogy if I ever heard one.

"Look," Calloway interjects, "If there's one thing I've learned, my friend, it's this: life is a series of moments. Some are good, some are bad, and a lot of them are really fucking twisted and generally beyond my comprehension. But every moment you spend planning for something to go wrong is one less moment you'll have, in the end, to make things right."

122

The cell block door opens, my name called.

I wrap my fingers around the bars.

"That's me!"

A guard with cropped red hair and a thin mustache approaches the cell.

"You have a visitor, and it's not your lawyer, son." The limp name tag attached to his green uniform identifies him as Barry. "You don't look like the type of guy I need to put in cuffs. Are you?"

"No, sir," I reply, "I'm just another guy whose Friday night took a wrong turn."

"Well, I can't take the risk," Barry says, "Just want to make sure you're not the type of asshole who's going to pull any funny business. Hands between the bars, please."

I oblige. Cuffs tighten and the cell door opens. Barry takes me by the thick of my arm, leading me away from my group of fellow misfits. Calloway takes my place, his head poking through the space between the bars.

"Stay strong, my friend!"

Sure thing, Aaron. I'll remember that when Claire brings the wrath of women everywhere down on my head. While she's reminding me why I'm the scum of the Earth, I'll be sure to remember to stay strong, just like you said.

I let out the stale air I've been holding in for too long.

To my surprise, great dismay and simultaneous relief, it's not Claire sitting on the other side of the glass. The bleary-eyed, pint-sized ball of fury I was expecting, a face of extreme disappointment and betrayed sobs, is a lacking presence.

Instead of my fiance, to whom I actually owe a real explanation, my contender of the night is the woman who put me here.

Taking my seat, we both reach for the black receivers beside us.

"Leonard," Mandy says, "this was nice, wasn't it? Not only did you have the nerve to completely shut me out of your life, but you thought I'm the kind of girl that give up on someone she loves?"

"What do you really expect will come of this, Mandy?"

"Fuck you asshole, okay? I'm not the one who decided he was too good for me after I offered him everything.I hope there's a nice, big bruise growing on that ego of yours, because if anyone deserves it, it's you."

"I don't need this right now," I reply, "You know whatever you've thrown at me won't stick, don't you?"

"I beg to differ," she says. "Looks to me like they're sticking it to you pretty good already."

"I got these bruises in a fucking bar fight."

She shrugs.

"Doesn't matter what I told them. Point is, they believed it."

"So that's it?" I ask, "You're just going to leave me here to rot, when I've done nothing to you?"

"Have you not heard a single word I've said, Leonard? Are you actually fucking dense?"

"Fine, you want it straight?"

"Please," Mandy replies.

"I couldn't give two fucks about you, lady. I've been running around, thinking I was doing a good thing. Thinking I was noble. Thinking I could save someone I care about. You know what I think now?"

"What's that?"

Skylar's words keep echoing in my head. I close my eyes and see the cuts on her arm that would become scars, were she to live long enough. I can see her dry hair and pale face and insurmountable challenges.

You're doing this to see how you are.

"I think," I say, " this conversation is over."

I hang up the receiver and summon Barry to escort me back to my cell.

Mandy can think whatever she wants. She's obviously not in much of a hurry to help me out of my predicament.

As Barry guides me down the hall and into the holding area, where Calloway greets me with a nod; as the cop closes the cell door and I'm left once again, staring down the clock, I can't shake the feeling I'm a complete fucking asshole. I want to yell. I want to laugh. I want to tell the world to fuck itself. I want to tell myself to fuck myself.

This is my fault.
At last, my brain and heart are in agreement.

Despite the men sleeping to the east and south of the tips of my shoes, I feel remarkably alone in the corner of my cage. Wallace continues to twitch throughout the night. Calloway grunts and snorts through his sleep. The biker, whose name is Lionel, lolls his head from side to side.

They bring in a couple other guys, but the cell block remains quiet for a weekend. Most of them are in here for mouthing off to cops, drinking and driving, or vandalizing the nice houses in Etobicoke. It's like a mix and match bin of misfits and here I am, at six in the morning, waiting for my life sentence like a love-sick puppy.

What is Renee going to tell Claire? What will Claire say when I come home from my current captivity and take her hands in mine, watching her break down as I try to rationalize the irrational?

What am I going to say when she finds me?

"Not tired, are you?" Calloway asks, offering one open eye in unwarranted support.

"Go back to sleep," I say, "it's nothing you can fix, Aaron."

He sits up on the bench, stretching his arms first, which crack as he rubs joint against bone; then his neck, which he rolls clockwise, then counterclockwise.

"Nah," Calloway replies, "Sleeping in this place is like sleeping on a fuckin' airplane. Every draft is like turbulence, shaking up your dreams. Cold and fucking uncomfortable, What I always say."

"You been in here a lot?"

Aaron chuckles.

"I've been in here enough. Let's leave it there. Like the ex-wife says; I get into the booze and become a different person."

"Been there. Done that. Ruined a couple good things on the way."

"Yeah, you look like you've been around the block a couple times, kid. Normally I'd buy you a drink and invite you to open the fuck up, but as you can see, this is no bar. More importantly, you seem to harvest a major fucking chip on your shoulder whenever I ask you something."

I smirk.

"That bad, eh?"

Calloway nods.

"Now honestly, I'm not going to sit here and pry it out of you. If you want to play it like you're fuckin' Mysterio, well, that's your business. But I know a tortured soul when I see one. And when we get out of here, you look me up. I think I can help you; just like I've helped a lot of other people."

"What are you?" I ask, "Some kind of lawyer?"

"Not quite. Well, I used to be a lawyer. But I was involved with some shady stuff on the side and I got disbarred. So now, I'm like the guy who gives you advice on the lawyer's advice. I know the system. I beat the system every single day, and I ain't doing it for eighty bucks an hour. I'm like the middleman of lawyers. To be completely honest, I piss a lot of people off. "

"What would such services cost me?"

"For you? No charge, my friend. The outcasts have to stick together."

"So what is it, exactly, you get out of helping me?"

Calloway looks genuinely surprised- the creased frown and the puzzled light in his eye come together quickly, as if my question has caught him off guard.

"Can a man not be a Good Samaritan these days?"

"Sure," I reply, "if you're trying to B.S. me that there's nothing you want in return."

"Maybe I don't."

"You can understand then, why I don't believe a word of it."

"Sure," Aaron says, "if you're trying to convince me all men are despicable creatures and are incapable of altruism; then you're entitled to believe what you want. But coming from a man who's been in my company all night and still hasn't voluntarily told me his name? You have to ask yourself; when do your beliefs start to have anything to do with mine?"

Questions answered with questions.

"Okay," I say, "I definitely believe you're a lawyer."

"Yet you still refuse to believe my reward has more to do with capital gain than selflessness."

"What can I say? It's my firm and undying belief behind whatever 'altruism' we're capable of, every man wants something for himself."

"Of course I want something for myself," Aaron says, "I want my son Jack to go to college and not end up a dawdler. I want my daughter Emily to stop dressing like she's the corner whore, and my wife to stop asking so many questions about my drinking. But I don't need millions of dollars to do so. Unless...are you suggesting corporate greed is the human condition?"

"No. Just... there needs to be some kind of material payoff for people to deem it worthwhile. Call me jaded, but it's where I stand."

"What? To want a house in the suburbs, a wife who loves him, maybe some kids who won't grow up to hate him? What about the itinerant doctor who risks life and limb every day to bring medical care to a poverty-stricken village? What about my pro bono colleagues who serve as public defenders in a justice system designed to protect the rich? The countless soldiers who die by the numbers to preserve the shaky balance that's democracy? There are people making a difference. What do you think they want for themselves?"

I'm sharing a cell with goddamn Socrates. Ironic, considering Socrates spent a small chunk of the end of his life in jail for allegedly corrupting the youth of Athens. I wonder how close Calloway has come to chugging hemlock himself.

"Alright," I say, "I'm sold. My name is Leonard."
Calloway grins and extends his hand.

"It's nice to meet you, Leonard. So you ready to tell me your story, or do I have to charm my way into those pants, too?"

What can I say? The guy can market himself.

I'm not a religious man. I've never invested in the idea of a higher power outside my personal rhetoric; never made an unadulterated confession to anything but a word processor. So opening up to Calloway seems impulsive and desperate; but as I jump from the beginning to the end and back to the middle, it starts to feel natural. Like writing the vulnerable truth on a concrete wall. Something, no matter where you've been or what you've done, which will not judge you.

The other men sharing our cell, with the exception of maybe Wallace and a scowling newcomer named Phil, are also listening. When Phil makes a smart-ass remark, Lionel the Biker shoots him a dirty look, and the snippets of backcountry commentary cease momentarily. This is a process which repeats itself because Lionel seems just as interested as Calloway, arms crossed.

It also repeats itself because Phil is a bit of an asshole.

"Fuckin' girl," he will interupt, "Grow some fuckin' balls."

At one point, Lionel the Biker slaps him upside the head and you can hear a small tap that should have cracked Phil's head into a wall.

"I told you to shut the eff up," Lionel says. "Told my old lady I'd give up the eff word but that doesn't mean I won't beat your punk ass down. Now- shut the eff up!"

Phil shrivels into a corner.

"That's what I thought."

By the time I'm concluding with Renee's confrontation and Mandy essentially framing me, even Phil has started listening. By the time they have finished processing my words and are whetting their lips to give me insight and responses and rationalizations- hell, maybe solutions- Barry comes to collect me.

"You've got a visitor."

I stand as tall as I can, shaking the sleep from my immobile muscles.

"Let me guess. My lawyer?"

"Is she short and blonde?"

Claire.

I slide my hands through the bars and look up at the clock as Barry fastens a fresh set of cuffs around my wrists. Once I pull my shackled hands away, he opens the door. There is no call-out of confidence from Aaron or Lionel or Phil.

I get a twitch from Wallace.

Instead, as it feels like I'm dragging my feet toward my executioner, it's Barry who offers me the most consoling piece of advice I've heard since I got here.

"Heard your story," he says, "Is it true?"

I chuckle.

"The part where I destroyed my relationship or the part where Lionel bitch-slapped the redneck? They're both true."

We arrive at the visitation center. Through a small glass window, I can see the ends of Claire's strands of disheveled hair, but not her face. I can see the cracks in her nail polish but I can't see her eyes. I need to see her eyes.

I just need to see her eyes.

"If you want my advice," Barry says, "Just come clean, Leonard. A couple years ago, I came within seconds of being caught red-handed by my wife. It's a secret I never had the courage to tell her, even after nine years of marriage and three children. But God as my witness, I love my kids. I stopped messing around, but I spend every day wishing I could tell her."

"Maybe now's the time to start," I reply, "For both of us."

Barry probably won't tell his wife when he gets off shift in an hour. He'll probably go home, let her cook him breakfast like she does every morning, and crawl into bed. He'll probably stare at the popcorn ceiling for a while, thinking about this very conversation and wishing he had the balls to rock the boat and become a more accountable human being in the process. I know Barry will not tell his wife the secret today that divides their tomorrow. He's got kids to think about and college to pay for and he's in no hurry to add child support to the list.

I know all this because that is exactly what I would do.

Not today, though. Even though my weakness will lend Barry feigned strength, his actual weakness is going to be one of the few things to carry me through this.

He places a hand on my shoulder before opening the door.

"Take all the time you need."

If destiny had a soundtrack, a little chime to be played endlessly in the background, predisposed to annoy me for the rest of my life; it wouldn't be carols of joy or anthems designed to uplift the broken spirit. It would be the flat, and excruciating, tones ringing in my left ear.

Not the sizzling of backyard barbeques and family gatherings playing backwards in your brain, but the sound of music on its deathbed.

Like a bee permanently buzzing around my head, the monotonous and maddening sound blocks out projections of poolside summers, winters in the Alps, every novel I may ever write. Caribbean vacations, retirement, even the thought of kids are wiped off the slate. The buzzing of my hornets' nest erases the weight of hopes and dreams because all I can concentrate on is swatting one bee out of existence.

Breathe, Leonard. Stop being melodramatic.

A loose white sweater drapes her shoulders. The air conditioning is too high and brings an unwelcome chill to the room. Only half a foot of plexiglass separates her and I; but it might as well be an ocean. Her hair is tied back and the makeup around her eyes is no worse for wear. It's what is in them I need to see.

I need them to gauge how hopelessly fucked I am.

I take my seat and reach for the receiver.

Maybe Renee has not told her.

Perhaps Claire will believe me.

Wishful thinking.

She reaches for her receiver.

We both wait for the other.

Say something.

Waiting to breathe, waiting for deus ex machina; for the mounds of cracking ice to split and drop us into the frigid ocean. Waiting for a perfect metaphor to come to me that will justify the things I've done.

Her shallow exhale accompanies her eyes fighting back a thin film of tears.

How much does she know?

How much of it is the truth?

Silence.

Breathe, Leonard.

"I guess I should go first," I say, "I'm glad you came."

As if it will stop her bottom lip from pushing into the top one, or the tip of her tiny nose lifting upward. Like it will halt the sharp rise in her cheeks or the creasing of her forehead, or hold blockades against the crying, which is no doubt coming, and the part I most dread.

"I thought you were better than this, Leonard."

She speaks slowly, regurgitating a conversation she must have played out a hundred times in her head. Trying to piece together fragments of information she has possession of; splicing together what slices of truth she thinks she's discovered.

"I can't believe what a fool I was," Claire says, "not to listen to Renee. Not to doubt your promises and your fucking assurances."

"Claire-"

"Don't!" she interjects, "You had your fun, Len, and I hope it was fucking worth it. You've lost whatever right you had to explain yourself."

"Renee told you, didn't she?"

Claire gasps.

"Was everything you said a lie?"

"Of course not-"

"Then why the fuck are you here? What the fuck have you been doing all this time?" Her breathing sharpens and shallows. "I thought I could trust you! I thought...if I could show you that you had nothing but my confidence, you would never have a reason to be dishonest with me!"

She raises her hands to cover her eyes and, weeping into her palm, the dam completely breaks. I am helpless to watch as contempt washes over her.

I look up at the clock on the wall behind my fiancee.

"And what's worse?" Claire spits, vehemently pulling her bleary eyes out of her palm, "I defended you, Leonard. All that fucking time Renee was on my case, Bonnie made her slightest remarks; all the subtle commentary from Mom and the rhetoric thrown in my face about you? I was the only fucking one to say, 'Leonard is a good man. He would never do this.'"

"Claire," I say, "you really have to listen to me. Renee doesn't understand what she saw! If you would give me the chance to explain, to fucking tell you what's been going on-"

"If you really wanted to tell me what the fuck you've been sneaking around on me for, with an underaged *child,* you should have done that before you proposed to me in the middle of a room full of people! You should have been honest with me from the fucking beginning; then maybe, just maybe, I'd be a little more lenient with you."

"Would you?" I ask, "Because it seems to me like you're so wrapped up in a fairy tale relationship, the fact it seems to be crumbling into the fucking Atlantic right now wouldn't have you listening to some bitch with a hard-on for tarnishing my reputation! So back the fuck off, okay?"

My poisonous word choice hits me before it even hits her.

"Sorry. I shouldn't have said that."

Claire scoffs. She wants to hide her vulnerability, but every facet of her being is exposed to a room full of knives, aiming for her heart. The shaking hands and the shaking head, the irregular rise and fall of her breaths beneath the cotton sweater; her mouth hangs open in utter disbelief.

"Claire? Look. None of this is what it looks like, okay? I can explain everything and it's really not as bad as you think it is. It's really not-"

"So," she says, "sleeping with numerous women outside your relationship is really not that bad?"

"I didn't mean it like -"

"Fuck you, Leonard."

Okay. I deserved that.

"And the fact you would resort to blaming Renee for your problems is pretty fucking low, too," Claire says, standing from her chair, slowly pulling away from the receiver in your hand. "Enjoy your weekend in jail. Maybe it will help put this whole thing in perspective for you. Maybe the next time someone agrees to spend the rest of their fucking life with you, you'll develop some fucking respect!"

"Claire," I object, "Honey, please don't do this."

"Maybe next time someone decides to trust you, you won't fuck it up like you fucked this up."

"Sweetheart, I can explain!"

Anger is a strange phenomenon. In one moment, the person you love and would do anything for; the person you would die for, disappears beneath the quilt that's fastened over her eyes. It turns people into a shell of their former self, and leaves you holding the razor-sharp end of the ropes in a decidedly final round of tug-of-war.

Suffice to say, the loving and somewhat naïve woman I fell head over heels in love with, in the hallway of a dilapidated apartment complex, is no longer in control of her emotions. Only her scalding, contagious tears hold her grounded in conviction.

"Claire? I love you, okay? We can fix this."

She shakes her head.

"We can't. You are....who you are."

Her bottom lip presses into the ridges of her top teeth. She's crying and I don't want to, but I can feel my own tears violently chugging their way to the surface.

139

All Hell is about to break loose inside.

"Goodbye, Leonard."

Despite my final onslaught of protests, there's not enough and time and space between her last words and the earthquake that follows the replacement of her telephone receiver on the opposite side of the glass.

"Claire!"

There's never going to be enough atonement to go around.

"Claire, come back!"

Her silhouette becomes another dancing shadow of the corridor into which she disappears, and neither ever look back. I call her name, and I slam the receiver in the cradle repeatedly until it nicks the end of my knuckles and a thin trickle of blood follows the dull throb coursing through my hand.

Still, I call her name and still, she doesn't return.

It's over.

I have to get out of here.

Being locked in a cage with my personal demons and a revolving door of new and old faces joining them is not doing shit for the anxiety that has firm grip around my throat.

I hope there's a nice, big bruise growing on that ego of yours, because if anyone deserves it, it's you.

I close my eyes, banging my forehead between the cold steel bars as I peer between them.

I'm dying, Leonard.

Skylar.

I spent my entire life convincing myself I was better off alone by destroying every decent relationship I ever had. I don't know much about destiny, Len, but I'm pretty sure the little voice in my head, looking back on everything, knew I'd end up here. It knew there was no point in planning for a future. On the other hand, you went after something that's better than what you are. You ended up pursuing what everyone else wants.

What normal people want.

I'm dying, Leonard.

Fuck off.

I let vision back into my brain; a collage of bricks and linoleum floors and future convicts who are the only company I'm worthy of.

I close my eyes again, and return to smacking my head against the bars, trying to inspire a train of thought which won't derail my entire life in the process.

I have to get out of here.

Luke's van pulls up to the curb of my apartment. My release was spent in tension, as a burly woman poured the contents of a brown envelope onto a dull gray counter behind a chicken-wire cage. She looked ready to go home, a smugness taped to her face and her sharp bun of thick brown hair on the verge of falling apart. I'm sure I looked no better so we both looked down at my slew of personal belongings- a nineteen year old wristwatch made by Swiss, a pack of winter flavored chewing gum, some loose change et cetera- because we didn't have the patience to meet each other's eyes.

I'm a free man, albeit a broken one.

In the passenger seat, I stare out the window at my apartment. My eyes feel heavy; my brain throbs with exhaustion. As Luke climbs out of the driver's seat, I reluctantly follow his lead. An elderly couple passes in front of me, both on walkers, as I retrieve house keys from my pocket.

For once, the door doesn't stick.

Luke remains several feet behind me as we ascend the steps. I pass the faulty railing at the top and around the corner, I'm greeted by a hallway that seems to extend forever. Each step takes longer than the last. From inception to completion, every time I lift my left foot, it's heavier than my right one. Like a death row inmate, this journey is spent dragging them to my front door.

I reach my apartment door. With trembling hands, I ready my key; it hovers in thin air before I slide it into the deadbolt lock and turn the handle.

The blinds are pulled, masking the walls and floor in a coat of darkness. The indoor summer air hangs thick in the foyer as the two of us enter, one by one. I don't switch on the lights or make a move to uncover the windows.

I don't remove my shoes.

Instead, my adjusting eyes pour over the living room. In my head, a crude inventory is conducted of things missing. I progress throughout the house, saying nothing. Checking to see what she took, for any clues where she might have gone.

I don't dare release the breath I've hoarded.

For every room I inspect, every morsel of clothing she's taken; for each suitcase that's noticeably absent from the hallway closet and each photograph removed from her bedside table, a familiar truth is dawning on me. It's simultaneously accompanied by an uncomfortable, deafening silence.

I'm followed by a ghost into every nook and cranny of my abode.

A thousand ghosts. Even Claire's missing toothbrush from the bathroom holder spawns a poltergeist of its own.

I return to the bedroom. Sitting on the queen sized, three hundred count sheets, I bury my face in my fingers as they slide towards my scalp. Oxygen is forcing itself down my airway, spurring panic. She took

144

the comforter, nine sets of shoes, all her makeup and her new summer jacket. She left her bridal gown but carried off with her photography tools and camera. She left her engagement ring, its centerpiece sapphire at an angle I'd clearly see it, glowing on the surface of her night-side table.

Against my weakest efforts, a dam breaks inside and quaking sorrow spews forth; a rush of violent emotion rocks my soul in a way it hasn't known since it was nineteen years old.

Coffee shops are the perfect setting for just about anything. It's a place where you can go on a first date with somebody, rendezvous with friends you haven't seen in too long, or break-up with your girlfriend because she wants a serious relationship, but you have other plans. It fits into the beginning, the middle and the end of any story. It offers security and operates relatively clear of plot holes.

Everything happening here unfolds in a natural way. It's an environment where everything can become exceedingly clear or unfortunately more complicated.

For myself and Claire, I hope the former will ring true but I have to be prepared for anything. After Mandy recanted her confession, the charges were dropped and I've not heard from her in the four days since.

Claire agreed to hear me out, not offer forgiveness. I don't know if the truth will bring her back and put her in that dress on a shiny white altar, but I have to hope.

I also have to account for the fact Renee will be here.

I'm not going to mince words or beat around the bush. There will be no half-truths, no omissions here. It's her word against mine.

The girls are together. Claire is wearing a white halter top and beige shorts which cut off halfway up her thigh. She looks composed, her blonde hair in a loose pony and several necklaces which fall to varying levels against her chest. Renee is, as always, overdressed for the weather in black pants and a frilly sweater. She

146

doesn't look at all happy to be here. Both of them are recent recipients of manicures and sport matching nail polish.

I see them, soon as I enter through the double doors of the coffee shop, sitting at a round table with three chairs. Claire stands when she sees me; Renee does not.

"Hey," she says.

"Hey."

"Your face is looking better. The rest of you looks terrible."

"Yeah, well. It's not been the most rewarding week of my life."

She squints as she studies me, trying to match my behaviour to what she knows. Trying to find the man she knows, lost somewhere inside himself.

"Can I buy you a coffee?"

I shake my head.

"No, but I'll wait if you want to get one."

I just want to get everything out in the open, and I don't really feel like delaying it just to stand in line.

Claire forces a smile and nods.

""Okay," she says, "I'm just going to grab something. I'll be really quick, I promise."

I sit down as she departs, leaving Renee and I alone. From across the table, the gum pops between her teeth, accompanied by a brilliant poker face.

"Hello, Renee."

"Leonard."

"Are you enjoying this?"

"Not at all."

"Neither am I. So how about you just admit you didn't see anything?"

"Well that would be fine and dandy, Leonard. Except I did see something. So how about you man up and confess?"

"Glad you agree. We're all after the same thing, you know."

More smacking.

"Are we?" she replies, "Because I find that hard to believe. I find it kind of funny- for all the shady shit you've been pulling, there's a credible explanation."

So do I.

Claire returns, cradling a white cup of dark, aromatic coffee in her hands. She takes a seat between Renee and I, bringing it to her lips.

"I hope the conversation didn't get too heated while I was gone."

"Not at all," Renee replies, fixated on my own stare, "You said you'd give Leonard a chance to explain. I think that's fair."

"Great," I chip in, "then you won't deem it unfair if Claire and I talk alone."

Renee chuckles.

"Oh Leonard. There you go again, thinking you're in a position to make demands. Haven't you figured it out?"

Claire's eyes close.

"Renee?"

"Mm?"

"Give us a few minutes, would you?"

She takes her eyes off me and addresses her sister.

"Sweetie, you can't trust your instincts right now. It's your emotions that are in control. How do you know he's telling the truth?"

"How does she know I'm not?" I ask.

"Leonard, be quiet," Claire says. "Renee, I'll be fine. Go grab a pizza slice next door. I just need a few minutes alone."

Renee looks between us, then reluctantly pushes back her chair. The gum-smacking stops; she briefly touches Claire's shoulder and leaves us.

Claire clears her throat.

"A woman called me. That's how I found out about all this."

"What?"

"She didn't sound very well. Her voice had this raspy quality to it. I didn't want to believe her at first, but she was desperately trying to get a hold of you."

Skylar.

"What did she say?" I ask.

"I needed to help you. I needed to be a good wife and help you to be a good husband. I don't know; she was crying a lot. Of course, I had no idea what she was talking about. I might have jumped the gun."

"So Renee never told you?"

Claire shakes her head.

"She told me I had to hear it from you. Said she saw something she probably shouldn't have, and asked

149

you to come clean. I was the one who overreacted. I thought whatever it is, it's nothing good. I have been played for a fool. It wasn't until the night after, I stopped acting out and started asking questions."

Renee didn't sell me down the river. For all her smug looks and cud-chewing, she's not half the monster she pretends to be.

Claire continues.

"So I thought you deserved a chance to be heard. I need the truth, Len. I have devoted two years of my life and I'm about to devote many more, but you can't hide this from me anymore."

I could tell her anything I want, including the truth. There's no longer a story to refute, an alternative narrative to counter, or contradictions to justify. Claire doesn't know anything more than what Skylar told her.

Skylar.

That woman has been more trouble than she's worth. She was afraid I would abandon her, and abandon her I did. In response, she did what she does best- stuck her finger in a socket in an attempt to shock everything around her into jumping to life.

"Leonard?"

I can say anything I want.

"Leonard, I need to know. Please."

Including the truth.

"You're too good for this, Claire. Too good to have someone who keeps secrets from you. I didn't set out to hurt anybody. But in the end, I always do."

Her eyes water.

"What does that mean?"

This is for the best.

"I was afraid being unable to write my wedding vows would make me a bad husband. But that was the tip of the iceberg."

"You're still not telling me anything."

"And I can't." I say, "because it doesn't involve you. I can't tell you the truth, darling. That's always been the problem."

She gasps, tears starting to stream down her cheeks.

"Why can't you just say what happened, Leonard?"

This is for the best.

"Someone came to me," I continue, "and changed the way I see everything. And it wasn't in an intimate way. Not even remotely romantic. But she challenged me to think, to live, to learn something about myself. It awakened something in me. She taught me to accept the things I can't control."

"What can't you control, Leonard?"

"This is the one thing I can control, Claire. I can save you from becoming like every other woman who loved me. You can get out."

She scoffs, shaking her head.

"What if I don't want to get out?"

I reach for her hand and take it in mine.

"I have to finish something. I don't have the right to ask you to wait for me. If you do, I will tell you everything when this is over. I promise ."

"Leonard, I don't understand," she replies, "What is so important you couldn't tell me?"

"You have to know- I love you more than anything. This is...this is just something I have to do for myself. Okay?"

She knows there's no choice in the matter. Pulling her hands out from under mine, she looks down at the table. Her gaze can no longer meet my own.

"Well," Claire says, "I won't stop you, Leonard. Do what you have to do."

I stand to take my leave. On second thought, I return to her and kiss her forehead, trying to capture a second of her scent I may need to ration the rest of my life. Pulling away, I don't look back. As I leave her bewildered and near hyperventilation, I can't return to comfort her.

Outside, Renee is returning from the pizza joint next door.

"So?" she says, "Did you tell her?"

I shake my head.

"Thank you for not selling me out," I reply, "She's going to need you now."

Genuine surprise.

"What did you do, Leonard?"

"Honestly, I'm sure she's ready to fill you in. Take care of her, you hear?"

I turn away from the coffee shop. Renee's stare pierces the back of my head, but as I get farther away from it, the feeling fades like a movie rolling into the credits. Between the mid-day sidewalk crowd, my step is abound with resolve as I head toward my destination.

It's time to finish this.

I climb the steps to Skylar's apartment thinking in a way, I'm glad the truth was neither laid out or hidden. I placed it where I'm most comfortable- in a niche of ambiguity. My punishment will be decided by me, the sentence carried out voluntarily. I've broken Claire's heart, but not in a way she'll forever spite me. There is still an open door we can mutually return to in the future.

At this juncture, though, I can't go through with the wedding.

Not before laying all this to rest.

I press the buzzer. It seems to be operating now.

It rings once. She picks up halfway through the second ring.

"It's Leonard. Open the door."

A chime rings above my head and the door unlatches. I pull it, perhaps harder than it needs to be pulled.

When we were younger, new adults relatively inexperienced in the ways of the world, everything was complicated. For every decision, there were a million little ventriloquist strings attached to our choices, and we made them for a variety of undisclosed reasons. No break-up had a clear cut reason. No girl I picked up at a seedy bar was without a stuttering explanation when I was caught by my significant other.

Now everything is black and white.

I reach the end of Skylar's peeling hallway. Bad lighting follows every step like a misguided sense of direction. I don't need to think. I don't need to circulate around a rat maze of reasoning and rhetoric. I don't know exactly what to say and what tone of voice to use. Whether to curse her or forgive.

I knock on the door.

Whereas I expect footsteps from the couch to the door, and a brief pause before she takes the plunge and turns the lock, there is no wait. The door is slightly ajar and pushes open against my fist. Darkness sneers between the crack. I reach out, fitting my palm against the degraded wood panel and gently push.

The living room is devoid of her presence. I peruse the wall beside the door for a light switch, my fingers reaching out for a slight plastic bulge. I find it, and the lit apartment offers something very different from the darker one.

There's no sign of Skylar anywhere near the couch or the television. Broken glass is spread across the floor, the coffee table is overturned, and picture frames have been ripped from the wall. Vases on the windowsill a week ago are now shattered on the ground, the flowers within lying in a puddle of stale water. There are holes in the wall and broken ceramic plates strewn across the counter into the sink. One of the cupboard doors has been ripped off its hinges.

I avoid stepping on broken glass and carefully make my way to the bedrooms.

Her sister is not here. Bethany's bedroom is the only undisturbed space in the apartment. In here, the bed is neatly made. The clothes are neatly folded. It appears virtually unoccupied.

Skylar's bedroom, on the other hand, is a disaster. Upon flicking the lamp switch, pieces of glass replaced by clothes, seemingly ripped from their hangers and flung at the walls, under which they lay crumpled in crude piles. A small cot has been turned on its side against the window. Blankets have toppled off the mattress onto the hardwood floors. More holes in the walls.

What the hell happened here?

Did somebody break in?

No. This is not the work of a break-and-enter. There's not a burglar in the world who would leave behind such a visible ruckus. You come, grabbing expensive china and jewelry; emptying safes and looking under mattresses for money clips full of cash. You leave, maybe having distorted an arrangement of cushions and left some closet doors open, some clothes strewn about.

Not even a junkie would be responsible for this kind of chaos.

Somebody buzzed me in.

Someone must be here.

She wanted me to confront her.

I leave the bedroom, shutting the door behind me. Resuming my tip-toe around the various grades of glass, from expensive to modest to bloody cheap, a sense of dread is growing. Unlike the dying flowers near the television, it's well-watered and tended to.

Maybe life is not so black and white after all.

There's only one place left to check.

The bathroom is located in the furthest corner of the apartment, beside the bedrooms. The door is slightly ajar, thick light pouring through it. I can't believe I didn't notice before, but that's the farthest thought from my mind. As I approach it, I see something between the crack.

A human leg.

"Oh Jesus."

Forsaking my slow movements, I push the door open.

The bathroom, other than Bethany's room, is the only part of the house not in shambles. The shower is covered by a red curtain; matching rugs and a toilet seat cover join the floor in painting a macabre scene. The mirror reflects my look of horror upon entering; it plays back my shallow breathing and dawning panic over a counter of neatly arranged beauty products and hand soaps.

Skylar is motionless on the floor, dressed only in a towel which barely covers her naked body. Wet hair, matted in blood, seeps from the back of her skull. I kneel beside her, pressing two fingers to her neck in search of a pulse. It's faint but fading. Her eyes are shut and breathing is shallow, her skin clamming and face pale.

What the fuck happened?

Keep it together, Leonard.

I turn her head and check the wound. The blood emanating from the gash is not self-inflicted. This is not the crimson bodily fluid of a nosebleed; this is a deep, dark red spilling through a blonde grapevine onto gray tiles.

Hands covered in blood, I set her head back on the floor and retrieve my cell phone. With a pounding heart and shaking limbs, I dial 911.

The operator picks up on the first ring. He asks me the nature of my emergency.

I wish there was anything natural about it.

"Yes! Hello? I came to my friend's house to check on her. She must have slipped and cracked her head. I need an ambulance."

"Stay calm, sir," the operator says, "and tell me where you are. We'll send an ambulance right over."

Panic.

I manage to stammer out the address. I'm given an ETA of five minutes and asked to buzz the paramedics in. He also requests I don't let Skylar out of my sight.

Believe me, I don't plan on it.

I disconnect, replacing my blood soaked phone in my jeans' pocket.

Back pressed against the wall, my spine somehow straight as it slides down to a seated position at her feet. The house phone is on the bathroom counter. I don't know who buzzed me in, or if it was a malfunction in the building's security, or if it could have been fate itself.

She had no opportunity to call for help. If chance was on her side, I'm not sure it would have occurred to her. Whether it was an aneurysm, or she fell and hit her head on the tub- possibly a combination of the two- she's lucky it's summer. Hypothermia might have killed her otherwise.

"Stay with me Skye," I plead, "It's going to be okay."

Behind a face slowly evolving in shades of blue, she has no condolences to offer. Skylar knew this was coming. She felt the changes suicide would have otherwise circumvented.

It's plain to the naked eye she wasn't completely at peace with her fate.

When my parents were brought into the hospital, everything seemed to stop. The emergency room has that effect on you. For the doctors, nurses, orderlies; it's a place constantly in motion. People are prioritized by the severity of their condition; stab wounds come before abdominal distentions, internal bleeding before nosebleeds. Loss of consciousness prevails over all else.

For people in the waiting game, the ER transcends space and time. Lives hang by a thread, doctors of every caliber hanging over your loved one.

For Mom, no matter adept her surgeon, it was a lost cause.

For Dad, no matter how poor his was, he would writhe between agony and resignation for six days. For almost a week, Luke and I alternated shifts, but there was always be one of us at his bedside. I read the paper aloud to him, a ritual from my younger days as Dad taught me to read. Luke would tell him stories about drinking in the ghetto bars and talk about his marital problems.

With severe brain damage, we were never sure whether he heard us. Seven operations and countless resuscitations later, he flatlined one final time. The whirring of the EKG slowed to a monotonous crawl, one that woke me from my dozing and let me know he had passed into the next life.

It took an eternity, but he was no longer suffering.

I enter the automatic sliding doors of the hospital through the emergency room. Following the yellow arrows on the floor which led me to the ER waiting room in the first place, I make a stop at registration. The triage nurse is in his forties, with a balding head and in blue scrubs. From behind his glass divider, a computer screen and a ringing telephone keep him constant company.

I take a seat in front of them as he's licking his thumb and filing through paperwork. He looks up after a moment, no smile or offer of welcome.

"Can I help you?"

"Yeah," I say, "I came in with a woman named Skylar Bates? She'd suffered brain damage and a fall. Does that ring a bell? It was around four o'clock this afternoon."

The nurse shakes his head.

"No, but I just got on shift. I can ask."

He starts to wave down his colleague when I stop him.

"No, it's okay. I was just wondering if her emergency contact had been tracked down. I don't know the family personally, so I have no idea how to get a hold of them."

"I'm sorry, sir, I'm not at liberty to dispense such information."

"Look," I reply, "a woman is about die. Are you telling me you can't even say whether the emergency contact has been notified?"

"That's exactly what I'm saying, sir. If she has an emergency contact listed, they have been called. If she doesn't, then they have not. Does that clear up your question?"

Unbelievable.

"You people and your bureaucracy. Just check in your damn computer and tell me!"

"Your tone is uncalled for, sir. I would advise you to calm down."

"How hard can it be? Go click, click, type. Skylar Bates. B-A-T-E-S."

The nurse picks up the receiver on his telephone. He lets it ring.

"Hi, Devin. Could you send security to triage? Thanks."

He replaces the receiver. A man using a walker rolls up behind me, his elderly wife lending him additional support with her arm. I notice them but I'm not clearing out until I find Bethany. The man is groaning and coughing and fighting his wife. He shouldn't be here and he's perfectly fine and he wants to go home, but his wife is hearing none of it.

I turn back to the nurse.

"You son of a bitch," I say, "Don't do this."

"I'm sorry, sir, but unless you're willing to step aside, these men behind you will escort you off the premises."

Two beefy guards approach me. The general waiting room population is staring at me. The nurses behind the asshole are staring at me. The world is watching like I belong to a circus sideshow, and I've made my grand escape.

"Fine," I say, "but I want your name. If she dies and her family isn't here, I'll personally make sure they know it was you who denied them the chance to see her."

"That won't be necessary," someone else behind me says.

I turn around.

I'll be damned. With his thinning hair neatly parted and sorely lacking the Hawaiian shirt in favour of a suit, Aaron Calloway is almost unrecognizable. He extends his hand.

"Nice to see you again, Leonard." He turns to the security guards and the nurse I've just finished accosting. "Thank you. There will be no need to escalate this situation any further, gentlemen. I apologize for my client's behaviour."

Security looks to the disgruntled male nurse, who nods his sullied approval.

They take their leave and I vacate the chair, allowing the hacking old man and his wife to take my place. Aaron guides me down the hall towards the OR by the arm. In his hand is a glossy black briefcase with a gold knockoff handle and locking mechanisms.

"Aaron, what's going on?" I ask, "What the hell are you doing here?"

He chuckles. We keep following the yellow arrows on the floor.

"Well, that is a story for another heated moment, my friend. Let's just say I have a deep investment in Skylar's affairs. Rather than going into details, I'd say it's better to track down her sister, hmm? Put this matter to bed?"

I stop. He stops.

"Listen to me, Calloway. I don't know if this is a some sick joke to you, or you have some weird fucking fixation with me, but you'll excuse me if I don't believe a word of what you say. Three days ago you were sharing a jail cell with me and quoting fucking Plato, so why don't you get to the punchline already? I've had a really long night, okay?"

I don't know what I expect his reaction to be, but it's not more chuckling.

"Man, you must have had some bad experiences with lawyers, Leonard," Aaron replies, "I'm Skylar's power-of-attorney. You can choose not to believe it, but here I am. I will admit, this is a pretty cool coincidence. I mean, not cool we cross paths again here, of all places."

"You're right. Not cool."

"I know where Bethany Bates is. Skylar listed me as her emergency contact because she was afraid to tell her sister the truth. I've already called Beth, and she's on her way."

"And you know Skylar....how?"

Calloway smiles.

"I'm an old friend of the family. When Skylar first called me, we hadn't spoken in almost ten years. She was a lost girl. She knew there wasn't much time, and asked me to keep an eye on her interests. Draw up her will. That sort of thing. Are you satisfied now?"

No.

"What other 'sort of things' did she have you do?"

"I can't tell you, Len. Confidentiality. You know the deal. I'm sure when the time is right, it will all become clear."

"You told me you're disbarred. You don't have the authority to do all that."

"No," Calloway says, "but doesn't mean I can't help. I'm just an executor. Skylar laid out her wishes and it's up to me to make sure they're fully realized. I have contacts she doesn't. I'm the guy who makes the magic happen."

"This is hardly magical, Aaron," I reply, "Fine. Let's say I believe you. What's the next step?"

He places his free hand on my crossed arm, beckoning me to walk with him. We turn a corner where the yellow arrows tell us, and follow the long hallway to the end. We pass scurrying nurses and patients; some sleeping on stretchers and others squirming in excruciating pain. Past gunshot wounds and violently sick children is another waiting room.

"We wait," Aaron says, "for Bethany to arrive. For the doctors to give us a prognosis. For this night to be over. Until that's happened, we wait."

"Okay, but what happens after that ?"

Aaron shrugs and takes a seat in the cheap blue armchair.

"Then it's in the hands of God. So grab yourself a coffee, read a magazine. Learn to accept the things you can't control."

I highly doubt God has anything to do with it, but take a seat beside him. Concentrating on my breathing, I try to quench my pounding heart and make peace with another night which seems destined to go on forever.

Bethany arrives half an hour later. As siblings, the Bates sisters look almost nothing alike. Her nose is a different shape, the eyes missing ever-changing gray tinges Skylar's have. Her mouth is wider on a chubbier face. Bethany's hair is black and she carries a heavier form.

Although we dated for two years, Skye's sister and I have never met before. The one time I had dinner with her Mom and Dad at a Japanese grill, Bethany was in Florida. Their half-brother Todd was present. He looked more like Skylar than Bethany does.

She recognizes Aaron instantly and embraces him.

I guess I believe him now.

"Tell me what's happening," she says.

"She's still in surgery," Aaron replies, "We won't know for a few hours yet. I'm sorry I can't tell you anything more. But on another note...Beth, this is Leonard. He's a friend of your sister's."

I stand and extend my hand.

"Hi Bethany."

"She mentioned you," Bethany says, "Are you the one who brought her in?"

"No, but I found her. The paramedics brought her here."

She wipes her eyes with a tissue from her leather purse. Her dress is casual; a red t-shirt and light black sweater. Old jeans and white sneakers.

"Thank you," she says, "I feel terrible. I should have stayed with her."

"It's not your fault," Aaron says.

"That's just it, Aaron. It is my fault. I don't understand why she wouldn't confide in me. She told me to leave her alone, and she was really....mean. Skye has said some terrible things to me in our time, but never like this. It bordered on spiteful."

"What did she say?" I ask.

"Excuse me?"

"I mean, what did she say to drive you away?"

Bethany hesitates to answer.

"Miss Bates," I say, "Your sister came to me after being absent from my life for a long, long time. Whatever your disagreements, this is not the time to keep secrets. We have to share the things we know if we're to help her, you understand?"

She swallows the lump in her throat.

"He's right, Beth," Aaron chimes in, "This is not something you want to hold in."

Thanks, Aaron.

"She told me....she said I'd been a terrible sister and I didn't deserve to know what was going on. She said I blow everything out of proportion and ...if I didn't leave, she would. It was almost like she would say anything to get me out of the same room."

She was trying to distance herself from every person who cares about her.

"But as long as we're revealing histories, Leonard," she continues, "maybe you can tell you what you two have been doing."

I cringe.

"That....is a very long story."

"Leonard, please. If you know something which might explain my sister's behaviour in the last few months, I'm open to hearing it."

"Is the fact she's dying not enough for you?"

"This is not the time to be defensive. Were you....you know, romantically involved?"

"Not that it's any of your business," I reply, "but no. Not recently."

"My sister is dying! Of course it's my business."

"Oh? I gave her the blood clots that brought us here? Is that what you're saying?"

Aaron takes his cue and steps between us.

"Okay folks. Time-out. Let's not create more work for the good doctors by giving ourselves a heart attack. No good can come of pointing fingers. This is obviously a very tense situation."

Bethany scoffs and paces back and forth.

"You know what, Aaron? You're right. So how about you tell me why you were called first and not me? Huh? Tell me!" Her face crunches into a ball and on the verge of an emotional breakdown, she says, "I should have been the one to get the call! I'm her fucking sister, aren't I? Doesn't that mean anything to her?"

I can now see exactly why.

"Please Beth," Aaron says, "Have a seat. Let's not get worked up over mere logistics."

"Logistics? Seriously? Is that what we're fucking calling it now?"

"Please, just have a seat."

Bethany shakes her head, and is about to reply when the double doors of the operating room swing open. A man dressed in aqua scrubs and a surgeon's cap emerges. In his fifties, he reminds me somewhat of my father, with the thick beard and piercing, exhausted eyes.

"Are you the family of Skylar Bates?" he asks.

Bethany steps forward.

"Yes. I'm her older sister."

"Hello, Miss Bates. My name is Doctor Halford."

"What's her condition, Doctor?" Aaron asks. "Is she going to be alright?"

Halford grimaces.

"Skylar has been in surgery for almost thirteen hours. One of the blood clots in her brain ruptured, leading to an aneurysm. The additional damage sustained by the impact with the bathtub has caused severe brain damage. I'm not sure we can repair it. We've induced a comatose state and will continue to monitor her from our Trauma Unit, which is one of the most advanced in the province. She was lucky to survive the hemorrhaging alone, but the outlook is bleak. I'm afraid there's nothing more we can do."

With both hands cupped over her nose and mouth, Bethany loses all sense of self-control. I'm not sure which is worse: the sobbing or the silence preceding it.

"I'm truly sorry," Halford says, "We're moving her now. You should be able to see her within the hour."

Aaron wraps his arm around Bethany and whispers something to her.

"Thank you, Doctor," I say.

He nods.

"I wish her the best."

Halford vanishes behind the swinging double doors as quickly as he appeared. People to see, surgeries to perform. Patients to save and comas to induce.

This is the place where space and time always comes to a complete stop.

I find Bethany outside the emergency room doors, sitting on a slab of cubic concrete. In her short fingers is a long cigarette. Half of it has been reduced to ashes at her feet. The other half slowly burns down to its equivalent.

"Mind if I join you?" I ask, walking up behind her.

She purses her lips, and only at this juncture do I see the slightest physical resemblance to her sister. A hand raises to her mouth and she draws on her cigarette, continuing to eat away at the paper which lends it shape.

"I'm sorry," I say, "I didn't mean to be evasive. I can't even begin to imagine what it's like. To lose a sibling, I mean."

The skin around her eyes is red.

"But listen," I continue, "What Skylar and I had ended *years* ago. There's no romantic involvement between us. She never really....told me the exact reason why she sought me out. Why she cared so much after all these years."

"Did Skye tell you she was dying?"

I nod.

"She told me. I knew when she was about to tell you." I chuckle. "Painted your entire apartment purple just to get out of talking about it."

"Yeah. I found that slightly odd."

"Slightly? I thought she'd lost her mind. But when I talked to her...I don't know. She seemed so lucid. Like she was privy to a whole different box of crayons. And when I needed advice on something, whether it was the

172

smartest thing in the world or the most monumentally stupid, it was her vision I followed."

"Which one was it?" Bethany asks, "Was listening to Skylar the smart thing to do, or the stupid one?"

I shrug.

"That's not a generalization I can quantify, Miss Bates."

"Meaning?"

"Meaning, I used to be a person who quantified everything." I search the horizon of university buildings and city lights. I don't need to find the perfect words, only a sliver of the honest ones. When the skyline offers none, I look to my feet for alternatives. "But I'm done trying to have all the answers. Trying to make a change."

Bethany stomps out her cigarette and immediately lights another.

"Sorry," I say, "but could I bum one of those off you?"

She turns the open pack towards me.

"Mm," she replies, "Take a couple. Plenty more where those come from. It's gonna be a long night so we'd better be well stocked." As I remove two from the pack and light one of them using her pink Bic, she tucks the box of smokes in her sweater pocket. "The devil, these things."

"You don't say."

The corners of her mouth twitch upward into a quickly retracted smile.

"You know," she continues, "I started smoking when I was fifteen years old. I'm near forty now. Our mum smoked. Two packs a day until she died at sixty-three. Alcoholism did her in. Always drunk. Dad is nine years older but he always looked better than her because she was always smoking and drinking. Always yelling at me and Skye. My dad was a pastor and a man of God but Mom? Atheist to the end. Smoking. Drinking. Yelling at me and Skye.

"Skye was the smart one. She never smoked. Never drank excessively or did drugs. But me, I couldn't handle that terrible woman. So I got hooked on these things. Being angry at my mother has been killing me for twenty-five years, one cigarette at a time. When Mom died, I drank a bottle of rum in her honour and smashed the bottle. When Skye dies, I don't know what I'm going to do."

I say nothing, allowing her to vent. Pulling on the filter funnels dour chemicals into my lungs and brings me certain peace.

"When Skye dies, I'll be alone with Daddy's dementia. Still sucking on these godforsaken things."

"Skylar never really talked much about your parents. I mean, I met them once. They seemed like good people. But she never really told me about all that."

Bethany shakes her head.

"It honestly doesn't surprise me."

"No?"

"Skye will defend Mom until the very end. Would have. Sorry; I haven't gotten used to talking about her in the past tense. Anyway, when our mother died, Skye was hit hard. For as drunk and loud and mean as she could be, they always had the better relationship. Whenever....I dealt with her, it I only saw the Hyde persona."

"I'm sorry."

"I'm sure you know she had the chance to get married."

"No. I didn't."

"Doug Wexler. They met in university. Even Mom was impressed by him. Daddy adored him. Doug was like the son he'd never had. He fit into our family like he'd always been there. After she left him at the altar, Dad was heartbroken. But that was Skye for you. Only thought for herself. She couldn't see the house and the kids and the two cars."

Sounds like the Skylar I know.

"That was after our time together, obviously." I say.

The smile reappears.

"Yeah? She never told me what happened with you two. By that point, she refused to talk much about romantic stuff."

"Do you want the long version or the short version?"

We both stomp out our cigarettes. She doesn't light another one.

"I want whichever version you want to give. Seems to me we don't have anything but time. Do you have somewhere to be?"

I do. The first cigarette left a craving for more.

"Did," I reply, "but I've done away with all of it now. No, I'm here to the end."

"Thank you, Leonard."

These things really are the devil.

By the next night, Skylar's condition hasn't improved.

The power of prayer eludes me. It's hard to ask of charity from an invisible man in the sky, with a flowing white beard and a bad track record when it comes to communicating with his subjects.

I'm praying for you now, Skye.

The rising sun pours through windows which don't open when my cell phone rings.

It shakes me from light sleep. I look up, remembering where I am when I see Skylar's vegetative state; a bandage around her head where only some of her blonde hair remains. Her eyes are closed and she's unrecognizable beneath the respirator, and yet indistinguishable from a girl I've known fifteen years. Wires running from her gowned chest into the heart monitor might as well be the tubes going in and out of her arm. A blanket covers her motionless body. Every once in a while, her legs will twitch, or her arm will jerk forward; her brain is sending baby signals to various parts of her body to elicit a response. Her brain is too damaged to realize it will never again produce a coherent state.

I just want to stop waking up from nightmares into another recurrent nightmare.

I was supposed to be married in a little more than forty-eight hours.

My cell phone is still ringing.

I pick up with heavy eyes, neglecting the caller display.

"Hello?"

I'm groggy, starved and inconcise.

"Leonard, it's me."

"Hi Claire."

"Where have you been?"

In a chair which makes every muscle in my back crackle and pop.

178

"Uh, it's complicated."

"Sorry. That came out wrong. I wasn't poaching. You said you needed your space and I'm still willing to give it to you."

"What time is it?" I ask.

"Five-forty."

"Oh. Have you been up all night?"

"Yeah," she replies, "I couldn't sleep."

"Funny. Me neither."

"You even sound stressed."

"Shut up," I reply, "I do not."

"You do. Are you?"

"Darling," I say, "you have no idea."

"Whatever it is, I wish I could be there with you. I don't like the thought of being separated from you. It makes sleeping harder. It makes everything harder. I miss you."

"I know."

"Do you miss me?"

"You know I do."

"Okay," she says, "I can deal with that."

"Okay."

"Bye, Leonard."

"Bye, Claire."

I pull the phone away from my ear, flipping it closed and setting it down in my lap.

Waiting for this nightmare to be over.

At nine P.M., Skylar flatlines.

The doctors and nurses evacuate Bethany and I from her room in the Trauma Unit. It starts with a seizure. Her body rocks the hospital bed and her arms flail for almost three minutes. The whites of her eyes appear from beneath their lids, and a nurse turns her head on its side. Machines go crazy with incessant whirring and beeping before a flat D tone replaces them.

The nurses wheel in a defibrillator. They shout something at the doctor, who shouts at them to pass him the paddles. From behind the window looking into her room, Bethany cups her hands over her mouth and pleads for them to bring her back.

I can barely hear them but I see them mouthing the words.

"Clear!" the nurse yells.

The doctor rubs the paddles together and presses them into Skylar's chest. Her entire body jumps at the volts of electricity surging toward her heart.

Nothing.

They boot it up for another run.

"Clear!"

Another jump.

The line on the heart monitor twitches and falls back to flat. I take Bethany, who says she can't bear to watch, into my arms. Together, we wait.

Come on, Skye.

"Clear!"

The doctor forces one last round of life into Skylar's heart. Her body falls limp but the machines return to their intermittent whirring and beeping.

"She's back," the doctor says, wiping beads of sweat from his forehead. As he emerges from Skylar's room, he turns to us. He's young, with blonde hair and a a checkered shirt under a white coat. The stethoscope does little to compensate for inadequacies at seeing people on their deathbed. His professionalism does nothing to mask his empathy.

"She may not have very long left, folks. Best prepare yourselves."

And, as he disappears, to another patient, another case, or possibly his lunch break, this revelation sends Bethany back into my arms.

Prayers really have no power.

I retreat to the lobby of the Trauma Unit. Taking a seat in one of the armchairs, I pull out my cell phone. It's still caked in blood from the back of Skylar's skull. With shaking hands, shallow breath and a heavy heart I press awkward fingers into the small buttons. I screw up a couple times and have to start over. The tremors spread from my hands to my entire arm as I lift the phone to my ear.

It rings twice before Renee picks up.

"It's Leonard. Can you put Claire on?"

"Where have you been? Claire told me what happened. We're worried about you."

It's nice she's had a change of heart. It's a thought I'll save for later.

"Please, Renee?"

Silence.

"Hold on a second," she says.

Muffled talking in the background.

"Leonard?"

"Hi, Claire."

"Honey, what's wrong? You sound terrible."

Keep it together. Keep it together.

I can't.

For Skylar.

"I'm ready. To tell you what happened."

"Okay."

"Can you come to the hospital?"

"I don't understand," Claire says, "Leonard, why are you at the hospital? Did something happen?"

"Not to me," I reply, "Please. I need you."

There's a pause.

"Okay. Which one?"

"General. I'm in the Trauma Unit."

"Okay. I'll be there soon."

"Okay."

"Leonard, it's going to be okay. Just stay put."

"Okay."

I hang up the phone.

I'm exhausted.

In the last three days, I've slept twelve hours, eaten six times, drank eighteen cups of coffee, smoked two packs of cigarettes and played a waiting game that feels longer than life itself. I've showered twice, had one change of clothes and cried or been on the verge of crying more than I can count.

I am officially and completely fucking drained.

I was supposed to get married today.

At three o'clock, surrounded by our family, friends, unknown guests and a city official that cost us three hundred dollars for an hour; with written vows in hand, little words would spell out what I expected from the rest of my life. If there's one thing I'm more terrible at than writing those vows honestly, it's public speaking.

There are a million reasons not to go through with something. Innumerable seeds of doubt grow into vines; they sprout and progress, wrapping so many of their thorns around conviction until the truth is buried so far beneath the rosebush, it distracts you from the flowers.

All my life as a writer, I've tried to control the things I can't change. I've tried to perfect the ugly truths of my life so often. All I succeeded in doing was making them uglier. Lies are the tool of temptation; readily available and always in abundance, but in the end all they do is push the good things away. In the end, the original idea is lost in a sea of supporting fibs that were required to keep it afloat.

Dishonesty is the devil's playground.

Claire arrives without Renee.

Indigo pajama pants and Reeboks, a t-shirt and cotton sweater. She made no attempt to look good for an emergency, fighting her own panic; I'm sure many different scenarios played out in her head. When she sees me, it's with relief too strong to mask.

I wait for her in the lobby where she embraces me.

"I'm so glad you're okay," she says, "What the hell is going on?"

I don't want to let her go but force us to separate.

"It's complicated," I say, "Please, have a seat."

We sit in the armchairs, facing each other. I reach for her hands and take them. Her fingers are warm in my clammy palms. The small, white hairs on her arm stand on edge, and blue eyes canvas my face for its little unwelcome emotions.

"You look terrible," she says.

Here goes.

I draw as much breath as I need.

"I lied to you, Claire. Over and over and over. I misjudged you. Clearly, you are the only person I should have confided in.

"My past has come back to haunt me in unimaginable ways. Every question begs another question. For every problem to be laid to rest, ten more pop up."

"You're talking in riddles again, Leonard."

Okay.

"Do you remember those phone calls? That Mazda parked outside our house?"

"How could I forget? I lost almost as much sleep over that as I have this."

"It was this girl. Somebody I knew a long time ago."

"Somebody you dated?"

"Yes. She came to me and told me about horrible things happening to her. Said she needed my help. I was having trouble writing my vows.

"I didn't want to acknowledge it at first. I can't say I readily considered it until this girl -Skylar- showed up.

"Before long, Renee started getting suspicious. I tried to steer her off-course, buy more time, but it only made her suspect me more. It led to some dangerous assumptions on her part. Everything started to spin out of my control. Skylar's condition deteriorated. Renee was shadowing my every move. Threatening to expose me. "

I stop and take a breath.

"And then, in the jail, I started to wonder what the point of all this had been. You would find out, if you hadn't already. I would lose the best thing in my life. For all the time I spent making sure I'd be happy forever, I already was. For all the time I was doing crazy things to make sure you'd always love me, you already did. I screwed up. Major. I'm sorry. If you give me the chance, I will spend the rest of my life making it up to you."

I cut myself off.

If I don't stop now, I'll go on forever.

"Okay," Claire says, "'You've said a lot. Not sure I can process all of it this second, but I'm not angry, Leonard. Seems we have things to work through, and a lot of late-night talks ahead, but this is not the end."

Thank God.

She frowns. "You still haven't told me why we're in a hospital, though."

"I needed you to have proof. I needed you to have more than my word, and show you. I can't do this without you."

"What proof, Len?"

I hold out my hand. She stares at my open palm, fear of the unknown rushing between her heart and toes. Scared my proof will forever damage her faith in me.

"I need you to trust me," I say, "Can you do that?"

She hesitates for a moment, then slowly places her hand in mine. As we walk down the hall to Skylar's room, she doesn't let go. Our steps are in sync, our hearts pounding at level volume. The white walls pass us like a blank slate. Anything could be written on them.

I stop at a thick blue door. She releases my hand, giving me the strength I need to pull the handle. It creaks on the way down, and the door unlatches from its frame.

I push inward.

The sounds of a fading heart greet her before the sights do. Skylar's face is paler than it was this morning, the vapor of her shallow breaths clouding the respirator. Her left eyelid droops lower over the socket than her right one does, as if the other isn't properly shut. The machines continue to whir at a seemingly slower pace than an hour ago. Dark blonde strands split and curl down the side of her face. She's ultimately lifeless, kept alive by a machine she never asked for.

Claire walks to Skylar's bedside, examining the idle hands and rhythmic heaving of her diaphragm. She studies my friend from head to toe, from the IV tubes protruding from her small wrists to the darkened bandage hugging her forehead. Claire hangs her head before looking back at me.

"This is her?" she asks.

I nod.

"Oh my God, Len. I'm sorry."

"Yeah," I say, "so am I."

"Is she going to live?"

"It doesn't look like it. Doctors say she could be dead by tomorrow. She flatlined an hour ago."

"I'm so sorry," she repeats, "Where is her family?"

"Her sister's here, somewhere. No real parents to speak of. She's got a family friend here, too. Interesting little fucker, he is. I'm sure you'll meet them."

She nods.

"I'd like that."

"Claire, I should have been honest with you from the beginning-"

"Len, it's okay. We don't have to talk about it now. Let's just...make it through this. You and I can wait."

She circles around to the other side of the bed, pulling up a chair beside the bed. Watching Skylar for any sign of return from the dead. There won't be one. So to bide the time, Claire takes her cold hand and holds it and begins to pray.

Maybe people hold onto their prayers because it gives them certain peace, instead of the preventative measures I always assumed they were. Just because it's unlikely to yield tangible results doesn't mean it's a useless last resort. If anything, maybe it provides a bridge between being broken and re-built; a road for the weary to spiritual wealth.

It was never meant for the dead, but those who are left behind.

Hmm.

Aaron Calloway makes his reappearance before Bethany does. His obnoxious demeanor has been wiped from the map; the man is all business. In a different suit with a different tie and his hair parted in a different direction, Mister Socrates himself has come to deliver the goods. No longer will questions be answered with questions.

Halford and another doctor accompany.

Introductions are made between Aaron and Claire just as Bethany arrives with her father John. The senior Bates is pushed by his daughter in a wheelchair, who explains although John won't remember this tomorrow, she thought he should be here.

"Where are we?" he asks.

Bethany tells him.

"Are we going to see your mother?"

This is who Bethany will be left alone with.

"I have some things to say, my friends," Aaron says, "Things Skylar wanted presented at a time of her choosing. That time, sadly, has come. We can all wish for something different; we can all tell ourselves there was something more we could have done. But it's not the case."

Claire takes my hand.

Bethany is solemn.

John asks if we're near the cafeteria.

Aaron sets his briefcase on a gray table at Skylar's feet. Unlatching the locks, it opens and he removes three letter-sized envelopes. A name is scrawled across each of them.

Beth.

Len.

Dad.

The envelopes are brown and it's impossible to see what they might contain, although I can make out small bulges in each one. He also removes a small laptop computer, presumably his, and a final brown envelope bigger than the others.

"What I have here," Aaron continues, "are Skylar's wishes and a package for each of you. I would advise you all listen to them yourselves once I've laid everything out on the table."

Bethany speaks.

"What exactly are her wishes?"

Aaron takes a moment.

"Your sister requested, in the event she flatlined and couldn't be brought back to consciousness, we are to let nature take its course. Frankly, I wasn't given an exact timeline, but I do know we weren't supposed to revive her. From what I understand, that's already come to pass."

He opens the large envelope and passes a single sheet of paper to Doctor Halford.

"This order effectively states we are not to resuscitate her. It's signed and notarized. You will see, these are the signatures of Skylar and her attorneys. I didn't present it earlier because I thought she still had time. This will free the hospital from any liability incurred."

"So what happens now?" Claire asks.

Halford speaks.

"That's up to the family."

A silence befalls the room. From her bed, Skylar's only words are the scribblings of the EKG. Her only voice is the moaning of a machine and the hollow breath bouncing within the confines of her respirator mask. She's completely unaware, free from the morality of this situation.

In a surprising display of lucidity, John speaks up.

"My little girl is going to die?"

This provokes a reaction from Bethany. The one tear she couldn't previously muster comes, rolling down her lifted cheek.

"Yeah, Daddy. She's going to die."

"What will your mother say?"

So much for progress.

Halford dismisses the other doctor. She's about ten years older, an expert at operating in the background. Within seconds of her leaving, it's like she was never here at all.

"I'm sorry, Bethany," Aaron says, "I let you down."

"Aaron, you did all you could." She looks to me. "I guess we should open those envelopes now."

"Yeah, okay," I reply.

I take mine when Aaron passes it to me. We share a tense look as he releases it. Bethany takes the other two. I stare down at my name, scrawled across the length of the paper in her handwriting, pressing my thumb into it to feel it out. There's definitely a bulge among its contents. Turning it face-down, I place my nail under the sealed adhesive and work it open.

On the inside I find, as Bethany does, a small blue flash drive. It's one those ten-dollar knockoffs you buy at the drugstore. My heart sinks as I hold it up to the light. In permanent marker, my name is written on it in small black letters; as if she was afraid to put the wrong message in the wrong envelope.

Nothing else.

"She only brought them to me a week ago," Aaron explains, "She said, should anything happen to her, she didn't want her last words to you spent in anger. Again, I would strongly advise you listen to those messages before you make your decision."

"Is that what the laptop is for?" I ask.

Aaron says yes.

Bethany and I look to each other. We're both treading water in the unknown. John may be a participant, but it's we who will have to decide.

"You should go first," I says, "I'm sure she would want it."

She dries her face with the back of her hand and approaches the computer. As the USB drive is plugged into the base of the laptop, it prompts her to open an audio file. A harsh exhale escapes her. Her hand lingers on the button before pressing it down and spawning a media player on the desktop.

The message begins with static before Skylar's voice, having taken on a raspier quality, preempts it.

"Hey, dork. Remember when I used to call you that ?" She chuckles. "It made you so mad. Mom would be running around in the kitchen. Daddy told us to work it out amongst ourselves. We never got to have the perfect family we wanted, but now I think if we'd been so perfect, I wouldn't have loved you guys half as much.

"I haven't been the most reliable sister, especially when it counted, but you have always been the greatest one I could have asked for. You picked me up when I was down. You never sank to my level. Even when I left Doug and couldn't tell you why, you were always there.

"I didn't want to push you away. And while you're probably blaming yourself for the way things turned out, there is nothing you could have done differently. Life is unfair, sweetie. If you take your eye off the ball for even a second, you're left behind. One day I woke up and realized I'm a hundred years behind the rest of you. As much as I want to live, as little as I want to die alone with my thoughts; well, death is a lonely place.

"I'm sorry for the things I said. You didn't deserve them. I know what I'm asking isn't easy. I'm secretly hoping to see me suffer will ease your decision, but don't expect it to be so. As inevitable as this moment is; I will always be with you, and hope you live your life as I would have wanted you to live it. Strong, proud and with your head held high. As I tried to."

There's a pause in the recording.

Skylar's fight for a few more seconds of composure.

"I will always love you, Bethany. Always, always, always."

Static returns, the recording fades to silence and breaks Bethany's dam all over again. Claire vacates her seat and escorts her from the room. Aaron and Doctor Halford follow her, leaving John and I in the room alone.

I don't want to hear words like that.

Get on with it, Leonard.

I walk to the computer, laying at Skylar's feet, watching her frail form speak volumes from beyond a premature grave. This is no way for her to live. This is no way for her to die.

John speaks.

"You have to be strong now, son."

Yeah. I know.

"I may not have all my faculties," he says, "but I can still tell my ass from my elbow on a good day. That's my baby girl in that bed, isn't it?"

"Yessir," I reply, still watching her.

Still waiting for a sign from God, if either of them are present.

"Then be strong, son. For Skylar."

He's right. I slowly remove Bethany's flash drive from the USB and insert the one I've been clutching in my hand since I opened the envelope. As it did with the other one, the computer prompts me to start playing the audio file.

Deep breath, Leonard.

Static.

"Hi, Len."

Pause.

"I don't even know where to begin," the ghost of her voice says, "Sitting here and asking myself whether I want forgiveness for the last month of my life, or all of it. If you can forgive me what I'm about to ask you, that will be comfort enough.

"By now I'm sure you're sitting at my bedside, or somewhere in lieu of it. Have you met my family? Seen why I avoided telling them? They act like I'm fragile. They did it to my mother as well. No matter what my sister's told you about her, she was the strongest woman I've ever known. In every bad situation, I tried to be like her. People used to tell me I'm my mother's daughter. Never knew what it meant until now. Impulsive. Self-destructive. A hurricane lives in me, and it wipes out the things I love. But I never wanted sympathy for it. I always tried to pick up the pieces and move on, just as you did.

"Beth will be not able to end my life. She's too emotional for that kind of burden. I only appealed to her because I need her to *let* somebody do it. And no matter how this might sound, there's reasons I sought you out. I wanted to make my peace with you. But another reason is your conviction, Leonard. You're the guy who does the right thing. Not always, but nobody's perfect.

"I don't want to drag it out. I could ask the doctors to do it but this is the way it should be done. This is dignity. I understand if you make the choice not to be that person. Just....if you have the strength to, you have my eternal gratitude.

"I'm sorry for the things I said. They weren't because I was afraid to die. It was losing you I couldn't handle. After all we've been through together, the fact I won't be there to see you prevail is my only lasting regret."

Claire appears in the doorway.

"Can I come in?" she asks.

I extend my hand to her and she joins me.

"...but in the end, I hope you will forgive me the words my darkness spoke, and use them to find your light. I hope you tell Claire the truth, because she seems like the best possible person for you. Better than I would have ever been.

"All I can ask is you display the courage you've shown me in the last month, and act in my interest now."

Claire rests her head against my shoulder. She tries to dispel her own tears but neither of us can.

"Stay strong. Stay proud. Accept responsibility for your choices, and always remember: I never stopped loving you Leonard. I will always be with you in every possible way."

I close my burning eyes.

"Thank you for everything."

The recording ends.

John asks when we're going the cafeteria.

Static.

Less than two hours later, in a series of seizures lasting almost eight minutes, everyone but the nurses, myself and Doctor Halford are swept from the room. The professionals shout at each other as the waves of ending life carry her out on the tides of death. Medical jargon is tossed about. Halford uses cues from Skylar's vitals to plan his next moves.

For eight long minutes, they try everything they can think of.

Bodily fluids spew into her air mask, forcing them to remove it. It takes two nurses to hold her down and prevent her neck from snapping.

I hope she doesn't feel a second of this.

When her body ceases convulsing, the waves of her heartbeat disappear inside a line that seems determined to drive on forever. With the crash cart ready, the doctor looks to where I stand alone in the doorway.

I shake my head and we're in unspoken agreement.

"She's gone," Halford says, "I'm sorry."

I don't look up from the floor.

Don't blink.

Don't speak.

I don't process.

She's gone.

Everything comes to a complete fucking halt.

Static.

One year later

My father once told me the measure of a man is not where he stands in comfort or convenience, but times of challenge and controversy. I believe he was quoting Martin Luther King, Jr.

This was one of his favorite lessons when I was eight years old; the kind all proud parents love to teach over and over and over. It's also the only lesson I remember this early in the day.

I wait in the early morning line at Starbucks for my coffee. The chatter of an indelible crowd is sorely lacking. The people in front of me are too tired to be my inspiration. The people behind me are too agitated at the length of the line that I would want it.

It's days like today I think of my Dad. He was a man trying to pay his dues to the world, to make it a less cruel place from the safety of sterilized operating rooms. Whether it was a medical conference, excess head trauma from hanging out in the emergency rooms of the General or a backlog in paperwork, those dues took their toll on our family.

Despite his shortcomings as a father and husband, I wish he were here.

When I reach the counter and an acne-infested, hunchbacked teenager takes my order.

"Just a coffee," I tell him, "Black."

"Tall, venti or grande?

"Large."

"So...venti or grande?"

"Gros," I reply, "as they say in French."

"So...?"

I roll my eyes.

"I go through this with you guys every time. The kids at Tim Horton's know what I mean."

"Leonard!" calls a voice from the end of the line. My grinning brother, sporting a new haircut and his best shoes, shirt and tie. "Nice suit! Stop holding up the line!"

I turn back to the cashier, my own grin creeping up on me. I slide a twenty dollar bill across the counter to him.

"Just bugging you," I tell him, "Venti. Actually, you know what? Make it two. Oh, and you can keep the change."

"No way."

"Put it towards your college fund. Hope your parents are paying. We need more educated minds like yours out there."

"Gee, thanks, mister."

He enthusiastically pours the two coffees from the red tap and passes them to me. I take them out of the line and join Luke, passing him one.

"You're looking good, Luke. Still shooting the shit?" I say.

"I'd like to know what shit you've been shooting. I mean, look at you! My big brother, all grown up. Looking spiffier than a spiff."

I chuckle.

"Wish I knew what that even meant. Say, shouldn't I have grabbed one of these for Monica?"

Luke shrugs.

"Not really worth bringing her a cold coffee, is it? C'mon, let's get the fuck out of here."

The woman in front of him is overweight, miserable and carries her equally chubby eight-year-old in tow.

"That language in unnecessary. There are children here, you know."

Luke scoffs in reply.

"Well, just think," he says to her, "the day your little tyke comes home swearing up a shitstorm, you can go right ahead and blame the fucktard who uttered a couple foul words in front of him. Like you've never told him to get out of the effing room, lady. Besides; what are you waking him up at six-thirty for? To pay for something you could make at home? It's those choices that will make him sign up for his first tour of duty. Mark my fuckin' words."

"Your mouth is appalling," the woman says, "I'm filing a complaint."

He rolls his eyes.

"Like that'll solve your problems. Let's go, Len."

Outside, Luke removes a pack of cigarettes from his pocket.

"You really are a crass son of a bitch, aren't you?" I say.

He lights the cigarette.

"What? The lady stepped in my personal space. And by that, I mean: she was a complete jerk! It's too early for bullshit! Do the math, my brother." He offers the open pack. "Want one?""

I shake my head.

"Haven't smoked one in almost a month."

"Suit yourself," he says, tucking the pack away. "Let's get to the rental agency. We gotta be there in less than two hours, Monica said."

"You know, the grammatically correct way to say that would be, ' Monica said we have to be there in less than two hours.' Just saying."

"Shut the hell up Len. Just because you're getting married this morning, it's not a free pass to bust my balls."

I think for a moment.

"Mind if we make a pit stop first?"

Luke groans.

"Len! We don't have fucking time for pit stops. What could be so important you'd let it delay yet another wedding?"

Don't worry, Luke.

This won't take but a minute.

"I know I haven't visited in a while."

The emerging blue sky is blocked out by overhead branches, whose leaves soak up light which seems to age this place a hundred years between visits. Gravestones in the sun's path are more prone to early erosion than their counterpart in the shadows of a lone tree.

"Sorry. There's been a lot going on. Moving, wedding stuff, life; you know the drill. Imagining you can hear me is a bit of a stretch, but if I absolutely have to; I imagine you'd be pretty happy for me."

This used be weird. Talking to a gravestone.

"I mean, I'm about to have a daughter. Who saw it coming, right?"

Now it's the most natural thing in the world.

"There wasn't much of a debate. Claire and I came to a pretty quick agreement what we'll be naming her. You would like it. We just had our third ultrasound last week. Doctors said she looked perfectly healthy from the outset, so there's a lot to look forward to.

"We bought a new house, got the hell out of Toronto altogether. I've been staying with Luke. Came down to collect him for the big day. Monica's already at home in Orillia.

"I think it was good we took a year to sort ourselves out. To have gotten married in the wake of....well, you know, what happened; it would have been doomed to fail from the start. But Claire and I are better than ever. I even know what I'm going to say when we're standing at the altar."

Now comes the hard part.

"I probably won't be coming around much anymore. Not because I don't want to, but we live so far away now. I'll be travelling a lot. But, um, this will be the last we see of each other. Not forever, just....a while. "

I look back to Luke, who's tapping his watch-less wrist and beckoning for me to speed it along.

"Well," I say, "I guess this is it. Take care, Skye, wherever you are."

I spot some sprouting flowers a couple feet away. Walking to them, I sever their roots from the ground and lay them on the plot, standing straight to face my old friend one last time.

"You're always in my thoughts."

I return to Luke.

"What?" I ask.

"Well, nothing. If you're not the most sentimental dude to ever live. Can we get going now? Monica will have my balls on a plate with her cake if we're not there on time."

"Lead the way, my brother."

As we leave the cemetery, I look back one last time, wishing Skylar could have been with me today.

Of all the people I've lost in my life, of all the people I claimed to love; when they left, it never made my life easier for their being gone. At least with Skylar, there was no internal struggle over that that truth.

Mom and Dad left a house and a gaping hole in the ground. It took two decades to a build my own house over them.

Our family has grown.

Renee and I are closer now. Under her snappy demeanor and bad fashion sense is a friend that tried to bring out my better side. Once I stopped resenting Renee for her tactics, I realized she's not such a bad person.

Kind of like Monica, whose endgame will always elude me. I suppose as long as she's my sister-in-law, I'll love her for what she is, and never what she's not.

Losing someone is never easy. The toll it takes can follow you around for a lifetime. If you're anything like me, you'll drag it around with you like tin cans attached a the back of a U-Haul truck. You let it fester until the right catalyst comes along and drops a match in a puddle of gasoline. If you're lucky, fire will burn the bad away and leave you with a clean slate.

If you happen to be the other guy who is not as lucky as I was, all I can say is "Godspeed".

For the first time in my life, mourning is a clean process. The birth of something new.

Destiny is a funny thing.

Acknowledgements

This was a book that took eight long years to finish. In that time, it went through many readings, edits, revisions and ideas.

I would like to thank the people who painstakingly took the time to offer feedback, perspective and constructive criticism. Sam McGraw and Sarah Wellington for the initial draft. My mother Rose for also lending her editing expertise to the final draft.

Kindra Austin for putting up with my incessant requests, only to grace this book with her wonderful foreword.

Kristiana Reed for her willingness to read my endless deluge of work. You are the best. Candice Louisa Daquin for a wonderful pre-release review. Jasper Kerkau and the rest of the editors who took me under their wing at Sudden Denouement. Members of Sudden Denouement for their endless encouragement and inspiration.

Sara Bambury for her input into key scenes. I adore you. Christine Ray for all her hard work with Indie Blu and Sudden Denouement, who indulges my constant badgering and assisted me in the panic leading up to release.

My daughter Skylar, who is named after the character in the story you just read, for inspiring me to go above and beyond every day.

My friend Michelle Vachon, whose untimely passing in large part inspired this story and so many other endeavours.

And you, reader, for supporting my dream and buying this book. Thank you for your support. It means the world.

Coming 2019

FOUNDING FATHERS

Preview

Samantha

Weddings are a bleak affair.

It occurs to me at the worst moment, too; in a sea of somber dresses and black cravats.

Statistically, marriage is far more likely to end in divorce than dying in each other's arms, but who are we kidding? Children were made to console dying parents.

No one better echoes that sentiment than my sister Stephanie, her tiny frame tucked into a plush red chair that matches the carpet but not the white drapes or the small oak coffin across the room.

She refuses to look at it. She sits across from me, chomping peppermint gum to cover up the half bottle of gin she pounded back on the limo ride here, glaring at our elder sister Laura, who has somehow turned this into the social event of the year.

Local celebrities. Activists. Sure I saw the mayor at some point, lurking in the corner.

Laura uses her warm green eyes and forced laughter to charm their minds, and a dress better suited for cocktail parties to woo men's eyes. Their wives snort at her when she twirls her hair, and scowl when she flirts with the husbands.

Not one of these people knew my mother. Her face, adorned on an old photo Laura had blown up as a stand-in for the open casket, shows her smiling. It was the only good picture we could find on two days' notice. It was only found because Stephanie fell asleep, her head in the family photo album.

If our mother were here, she would kick half these people to the curb. Tom and Corey, one my senior and the other, five years junior, stand off to the side of the room, talking quietly. Tom is a young Dean Martin in his pressed suit, while Corey, with his shaved head and hastily assembled attire, could have slept in his.

We all know Laura has hijacked this event. Her husband Paul does his best to restrain himself from pulling his wife off her promiscuous tour of the funeral-going elite.Her kids, Jacob and Reese, roll their eyes when required and go back to their handheld video games at their leisure. Eventually, Paul gives up on my sister's dignity and wanders away to save his own.

Specifically, towards Stephanie and I.

"You two look like you haven't slept in a week," he says, taking a matching armchair. "We ate at this amazing, high-end restaurant last night. Vinny's. Little Italian place that just opened up downtown. Slept like a baby after that meal, I tell ya."

Stephanie squints, a perfect mixture of annoyance and disgust. "Not all of us live a posh life, honey. Some of us live in the real world."

"Ignore her," I tell him, "She's just mad because Laura is making a joke out of this thing. Am I right, Steph?"

"I understand," Paul says, "Losing a parent is never easy. You got resentment, you got the squabbling. Blah, blah. I get it. I do."

"And how's your mum, Paul?" she shoots back.

"Mom's great! Playing golf in Florida, blowing the docs off about her cholesterol, but you know, it's all about the living. I swear, that woman has, like, at least three guys on the go at any time."

Stephanie rolls her eyes.

"Just shut up. And gross."

"The woman will outlive me at this rate. Which, is probably bad taste, since we're at a funeral."

"Seems like a good time to stop talking," she says, "Or maybe you could go tell my sister that guy she's hanging off of? Yeah, his wife looks pretty angry."

With Paul gone, she turns her blank stare back to the wall.

"You okay?" I ask, "Seemed kind of short there."

"Please," Stephanie says, "You want to ask that question even less than I want to answer it."

"You're right, because it seems you're only at peace sucking on the end of a bottle in a paper bag at this point. You can't do this all alone."

"You forget, Sam. I've been doing this all alone. Who sat with Mom during all the treatments? Who sat with lawyers and banks, went through trusts and funeral plans and estates and more bullshit than the four of you have ever gone through for her? Who had to listen to the insults and misery and fucking slurs? When was the last time Mom called you a whore in her sleep, when you were sitting right there next to her?"

"Sorry," I say. She sighs. Has not looked me in the eyes. Probably to keep the tears out of her own. "It wasn't fair you got stuck with that."

"It's fine, Sam. Should have known it would happen."

"Least you didn't have to deal with *him*," I say. It's a small comfort, but the best I can offer her. "God knows how that would have gone."

She chuckles. "I would have ripped him a new one, likely. Last time we spoke, he was congratulating me on my first divorce. Motherfucker."

"That's appropriate," I chide.

"When was the last time you spoke to him?"

"Hmmm?"

"Dad. When did you speak to him last?"

I want to tell the truth, but don't dare.

"About a year ago. Derek had just left me for that...*person* from Bermuda. Wrote me a check and disappeared in the night. Dad called, asking how I was. Thought he was my real estate agent."

"You always were dumb, sis," Stephanie says.

"He was asking more questions about Laura than he was about Derek. Nathan was still largely in the dark. I didn't have time for Dad's shit. Hung up on him and cried into a bottle of red. Complete meltdown that night."

Until he called me a year later, I want to finish. The night my mother died.

215

"What the flying fuck is wrong with men? Can they not just keep that thing in their pants?" She holds her bent pinky finger up to personify it.

"I don't have one, or I'd tell you, Steph."

Across the room, Laura calls everyone to attention, clinking her stemmed glass of water with a plastic fork. She always was inefficient.

"Time for the eulogy, I guess," I mutter. "You ready?"

"To put this bag of bones in the ground? You bet."

The pulpit feels smooth under my shaking hands. I have rehearsed my part a couple thousand times, but I forget all of it now. After listening to my brothers, trying to conjure any happy memories they can salvage into coherent tributes, then Laura, making light of it all, I don't even want to speak until the nausea subsides.

Stephanie's eulogy is bitter, and I know I can't let my mother be laid to rest on such a note.

"My mother didn't want a funeral," I admit to the crowd. Looking into a sea of beady eyes and fake complexions, uncomfortable postures and tapping feet, the words are Moby Dick, fighting back. "She would not have even wanted this wake. She couldn't stand me, her middle born. Told me I would end up on some corner, peddling heroin or pussy. No joke.

"She didn't love Laura, who she treated like a doll. Avoided Corey because she hated the smell of pot. And Steph, who just wanted to be loved, unlike the rest of us; well, Catherine hated her too.

"The only one she probably did show affection to, at some point, was my brother Tom, who is also the only of us that turned out normal."

Laura sneers in the front row, clasping onto Paul's hand for support during the wave of uncomfortable chuckling.

"She would have definitely told you all to shove off if she saw you here, because that's who my mother was. A woman hurt too many times, stripped of her emotions like rocks in a coal mine. The last time I spoke to Catherine, she asked me if I was gonna get sewn up because my husband left me. I retorted something equally pleasant, and the rest is history.

"She knew life would never get any better and avoided it. And here I am, flailing like a bird with broken wings in the wind just trying to wrap my head around that."

My name is Sam, and I'm not an alcoholic. Just a basketcase with bottles of merlot hidden all around my house.

"Obviously I came up here to sound less miserable than my little sister did, but there you have it. I'm not. She gave me many gifts, but happiness was never one of them.

"Rest in peace, Mom."

Life is a bleak affair.

One minute, you have it all. A house where the bills get paid, the lights stay on, the husband stays faithful. One minute, the future is locked down, the retirement savings getting built, and the kids are alright.

Easy how that can all be undone in a five-minute conversation about a bitch from the islands.

My messages are full, the cat is hungry, and shoes obscure the landing of my condo. Two floors up, the familiar roar of video games heaves along, making my ears pop.

Yelling at my son to preserve his hearing until after college, I hit play on the messages. The cat, an overweight tabby named Yukalaylee, incessantly begs me to fill his silver dish.

Norman, my lawyer from Pittsburgh, rattles off about a fight he had with the estate guy. I know Catherine had nothing to her name after ten years of disability and another three after getting sick.

"Yuke, relax!" I tell the tabby. He growls defiantly and rubs against my leg. "Nathan, I told you to feed him," I grumble.

Next message. My mechanic Gus, telling me the shitbox is up for an oil change. Another person looking for a payday.

Sorry honey, it will have to wait another month. Then, as if he hears my thoughts, a warning about not coming to see him. *Don't start another car fire, Sam.*

Next message. Laura.

Skip it.

Next message. Stephanie.

Next message.

"Hi, Sam."

Patchy. Like a broom sweeping gravel. My father, who called me last Wednesday, the night Catherine died.

"Um, it's me. Your Dad. Been trying to call you, but I keep getting through to the sound of a screaming cat or something."

I chuckle. *Dammit, Nathan.*

"Anyway, I just wanted to say I'm sorry about your mother. She was...well, she was a strong-willed person, and she gave me strong-willed children. I know I'm very late with this call; God knows. If you ever want to grab a coffee and we can exchange memories....or something!"

God, I think, *he's so awkward.*

"Anyway, I went to the doctor last week, and he said something came up on the blood test, so I'm penciled in for an MRI next month. I was just wondering if you could come with me, you know, because I'm a little short on cash-"

There it is.

I press stop on the machine. There are three more messages. Three more people lining up because I am the bank of Sam.

"Yuke!" I hiss at the incessant feline. He hounds my heels as I open the overhead cupboard and pull down a crumpled blue bag. He knows. Showing him the packaging is the domestic pet equivalent of bullfighting.

Downstairs, the doorbell rings. I drop the star-shaped kibble into Yuke's bowl, watch him collapse into the beginnings of food coma. Satisfied he will remain preoccupied, I descend the many landings of my condo to see who the hell has descended on my doorstep.

A young girl wearing a cream coloured scarf around her head occupies my front lawn, hugging a covered glass bowl.

"Hello there," I say to her, "can I help you?"

The girl smiles, but her hazel eyes are a dead stare. "Hello, missus. We just moved in next door.."
I had seen the long van earlier in the week back. I may have yelled at the young movers who, in a past life, would have appealed to me, even blocking said driveway as I was trying to get my son to a dentist appointment. The muscles, the sweating, the grunting as they navigated furniture with price tags still hanging off them through the other side of my semi-detached condo, would have gotten young Samantha's hormones racing.

Old Samantha, feeling used, washed-up and relegated to her shit circumstances, offered a tire slashing.

"Oh hi sweetie, nice to see you again. I'm Sam. What's your name? I didn't catch it the other day."

"I am Nadia. There's Iza, my mother; my uncle Farhad and father Omar, but Father does not move or speak."

"So your father is in the wheelchair?"

"Yes," the girl replies, "but you should never speak to him or my mother. If you need to speak to one of them, speak to Farhad, please."

"Well, welcome to the neighbourhood, Nadia. And thank you so much for the food!"

"Oh no," Nadia blushes, "these are not for you. This is dinner for my family. I am sorry if I misrepresented."

"Oh no," I echo her, "How presumptuous of me. I am sorry. Please tell your family we are very happy to have you here. Enjoy your stay!"

I shut the door.

I am such an embarrassment. Yukalaylee stares from his perch on the stairs, clearly in agreement.

Peter

It only takes a single moment, one of millions in the fabric of time, to realize you don't give two fucks about your fellow human beings.

Yes, it could be one o'clock at your local supermarket on a Saturday afternoon. You want to reach over the sagging woman smacking her husband with an ebony cane to grab that last flat of pork, circumnavigate the guy who helps you understand why airlines make people like him have to buy two seats, just to grab a loaf of bread and escape this bloodcurdling showcase of spoiled children and even more entitled adults.

For the young lady on the register, it's a life sentence until five p.m. She begrudgingly passes the same items over the scanner, sometimes hundreds of times a day. Her pout is unsympathetic to judging eyes that claim a stake in dead chickens and wilting heads of lettuce. Some try to make small talk with her. Topics range anywhere from weather to sexual harassment.

This is one of many places I come out of ritual, if only as a reminder that the President could start firing nukes around the globe tomorrow, and my only disappointment would be missing swaths of these creatures wiped out before my eyes.

I wonder if the girl on the register would agree. As long as her nails did not break, it would probably be welcome to her, too.

I have rarely been in love, but a lot of people around me suck at it.

My parents sucked at it.

My sister is bad at it.

My brother's love life is non existent.

My tenth grade math English teacher went through a very public divorce. Everyone in school was talking about it for weeks.

People talk about love like it's make-or-break. Like it's material success. Like, you want to be the OG Love, but in reality you have a person within arm's reach you can beat down until they are a shell of themselves, trying to fit them into your perfect fucking box.

My great-grandparents didn't have to choose love. It was chosen for them. He was a farmer's son. She was a cattle rancher's daughter. Love was transactional, a promise of marriage for some new mares or cattle. They spent decades together before they heard about divorce, but by then, were almost dead anyway.

My father was the business type. My mother was... well, his third wife. He was never home, but had a new secretary pick him up for each trip. One of those secretaries, a blonde named Mary, had loose lips. Mom found out at a Christmas party. After that, we only saw Dad's name on child support cheques. Those bought her new liquor cabinets and a boyfriend named Doug. When the money dried up, Doug wasn't Dad, and both were gone.

The only people I know who don't suck at love are Vic and Sydney, mostly because they don't give a shit about love.

She works at a corner store during the day, selling underage kids cigarettes after midnight, swapping between serving customers and her flask of mystery booze.

He deals pot from his living room, talking trash on the Internet about hard working American citizens and watching subscription cable. Vic sleeps with a gun in his nightstand, but he tells me it's for Syd, in case she ever comes at him with a knife.

It only takes a single moment to realize that all the potential your parents promised you culminated in you hanging around a convenience store with a mouthy clerk waiting to sell drugs.

Sydney is on the bottom of totem poles for merchants of death. Cigarettes and alcohol in an official capacity, weed and the occasional heroin under the table. Over the counter drugs are in the third aisle. She will tell you cigarettes are terrible while selling them to you, and hand out smokes to underage kids on her five-minute break. She accepts bribes as identification from school kids and relabelled the penny donation tray "take a fuck you, leave a fuck you".

"If you're not gonna buy anything, wait outside, jackass."

"C'mon, Syd," I say, "it's hot as balls outside. Plus, there's a bunch of weirdos out there."

"Where weirdos belong," she says. "Buy something or skedaddle, Pete. Cops come in for coffee, you're loitering and that makes you my business. Don't need questions I can't answer."

"Just show them your tits."

Syd sneers. She's small, like a child, and I'm sure she has never worn adult clothes, for as long as I've known her.

"Funny," she replies, "So funny, I should string you up and beat you to death with your comedy career. Take a fucking hike, Pete. Do my boyfriend's business outside."

Knowing better than to argue with her, I put down the magazine I've been flipping through and walk past
her.

If I knew this is what life would turn out to be, I would have asked my mother to abort me.

Outside is a sauna, and I can feel the air-conditioned comfort of the corner store vacating my body as I vacate it. Two elderly men in pork-pie hats sit outside a dingy cafe to my left, sipping tea and ignoring the world around them. To my right, a couple fellows named Jason and Rob peddle pot to innocent bystanders.

"Getch'yo dank here, good sir!" the lanky adolescent in a wifebeater professes, and to nobody in particular. His arms are thin, the rest of him thinner. His partner is shorter, wider and of fewer words, but he nods enthusiastically.

"C'mon guys," I say, "You're small-time. Don't try and offload your dirt weed on me."

The loud one, Jason, scoffs. "Hey bro, you know, I resent that sorta shit, 'less you're willing to smoke me a fat blunt and show me big-time, but nah, I guess you're just gonna walk away, and leave us mortals here to tend God's feces, ain't that shit right?"

Saying nothing, I pull a smoke from my jacket and light it. This guy should have been here by now. Instead, I have these two degenerates for company. I didn't even want to leave my house today.

"You know," Jason says, "Hear there's some hush hush going on with your boy Vic."

"Wouldn't know," I reply, "Haven't heard anything."

"Whoa, hold up. You mean to say we see you coming down here every day, pushing *mota* for this guy, and he don't tell you nothing?"

"When it's important, I'm sure he'll tell me."

I exhale those words like cigarette smoke, heavy and labored.

"Word around the neighbourhood is he's holding nightly meetings at the warehouse on Lord Street. All white guys, some skinheads, business types, biker dudes. Now I'm the same colour as their shitkickers, so I see a bunch of cracker-white brothers all heading into a dark building together, I'm thinkin' they ain't having brunch or some shit, ya know?"

So that's where Vic has been disappearing to, lately.

"Maybe they're playing poker."

"Could be. Could be. But *then* I get wind that Rupert Smith's at some of them meetings- yeah, that racist motherfucker- and get this. Cat's running for governor. All that that dough he got lying about from his telecom days."

"And you don't think it's a coincidence?"

"Motherfucker, who said coincidence? You got this mogul who owns half the weed operations in the northeast, has gangsters in his pocket from here to Jersey, running for governor. He hangs out with more white-collar killers than civilians, got friends in Wall Street, and is holding some covert shit on Lord Street with your boy Viktor. After ten p.m. Motherfucker, if I was out after ten p.m., the cops in this town would lock me up!"

Robert, his stockier friend in a trenchcoat, nods in strong agreement.

"Look, man," Jason says, "I dunno what Vic tells you and don't, but as a visible minority in this backward-ass place, I should tell you I ain't comfortable when I see shit like that. I ain't no expert in nothing but standing on this corner selling dope and getting harassed by pigs, but I know exclusion when I see it, and Rupert Smith is bad fuckin' news, homie. Should talk some sense into your boy."

227

I haul on the dead end of my cigarette and pitch it at the sewer grate. It bounces off the bars, rolling away in the heat like a tumbleweed.

The guy shows up ten minutes later, and hands me a crumpled hundred dollar bill. I give him the drugs, and he's on his way.

Syd emerges from the store, smoke and lighter in one hand and a black coffee in the other. After locking the door, she takes a seat at the curb and beckons me over to her.

"I see those two sadsacks left," she says, gesturing to where Robert and Jason were standing. "Finally ran out of fertilizer to sell, I guess."

"Actually," I reply, "they felt like getting pizza."

Syd rolls her eyes, lighting her smoke and taking a long gulp of the coffee. A thick plume of menthol cigarette smoke wafts through my senses.

"I don't know how you can defend people like that, Pete. All they do is push drugs and start fights."

"Yes, but to be fair, all I do is push drugs and start fights, too. Not the fights, so much. Sometimes, maybe. But it would be hypocritical of me to judge, wouldn't it? I'm just like them, not any better because of skin colour."

Syd scoffs. "Fuck that. White people founded this country. Our taxes built this country. My daddy worked every day of his adult life, along with millions of others, to make this country great."

228

"I'm guessing you've been going to those meetings on Lord Street, huh?"

Her sour demeanour turns even more bitter.

"Who told you about that?"

"Little birdie."

"Was this little birdie a person of colour who happens to stand outside my place of employment all day, hucking marijuana and stupid rumours?"

"Could be."

"Don't worry about it, Peter. And don't tell Vic you know. If he hasn't told you, clearly you're not ready." She extinguishes her cigarette on the pavement between her sneakers and stands up. "When you're ready to know, you'll know."

"Know what?"

Syd ignores the question, and unlocks the door.

"Don't keep Vic waiting for his money, Pete."

About the Author

Nicholas Gagnier is a Canadian writer and poet from Ottawa, ON. He has released three full books of poetry and is working on FOUNDING FATHERS, a novel to be released in 2019.

Lightning Source UK Ltd.
Milton Keynes UK
UKHW010211081020
371205UK00006B/151

9 781643 704838